CAROLINE STARR ROSE

Blue
Birds

PUFFIN BOOKS

To Jamie C. Martin

PUFFIN BOOKS
An imprint of Penguin Random House LLC
375 Hudson Street
New York, New York 10014

First published in the United States of America by G. P. Putnam's Sons,
an imprint of Penguin Group (USA) LLC, 2015
Published by Puffin Books, an imprint of Penguin Random House LLC, 2016

THE LIBRARY OF CONGRESS HAS CATALOGED THE G. P. PUTNAM'S SONS EDITION AS FOLLOWS:
Rose, Caroline Starr.
Blue birds / Caroline Starr Rose.
pages cm
Summary: "As tensions rise between the English settlers and the Native peoples on Roanoke Island, twelve-year-old Alis forms an impossible friendship with a native girl named Kimi"—Provided by publisher. Includes glossary and historical notes.
Includes bibliographical references (page).
ISBN 978-0-399-16810-9 (hardcover)
1. Roanoke Colony—Juvenile fiction. 2. Roanoke Island (N.C.)—History—16th century—Juvenile fiction. [1. Novels in verse. 2. Roanoke Colony—Fiction. 3. Roanoke Island (N.C.)—History—16th century—Fiction. 4. Friendship—Fiction. 5. Lumbee Indians—Fiction. 6. Indians of North America—North Carolina—Fiction.] I. Title.
PZ7.5.R67Blu 2015
[Fic]—dc23
2014012100

Puffin Books ISBN 978-0-14-751187-4

Design by Richard Amari

Printed in the United States of America

7 9 10 8 6

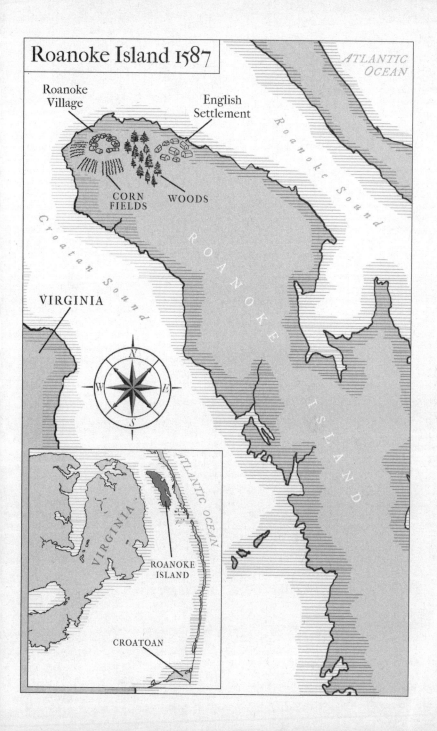

Roanoke Island 1587

Roanoke
Village

English
Settlement

CORN
FIELDS

WOODS

VIRGINIA

Croatan Sound

Roanoke Sound

ATLANTIC
OCEAN

ROANOKE ISLAND

N
W E
S

VIRGINIA

ATLANTIC OCEAN

ROANOKE
ISLAND

CROATOAN

July 1587

Alis

Almost three months we've journeyed,
each wave pushing us farther
from London,
every day moving us closer
to Virginia.

But now we're anchored on sandy banks
in a place we're not to be.

The enormity of our circumstance
comes crashing down around us.
Though this is Virginia,
it's not our new home.

We will be forced ashore
miles from where
our pilot, Ferdinando,
promised to take us.

Yet our Governor
does nothing to stop him.

Alis

How ready I am to leave this ship,
stretch my legs, be free!
But not like this,
tossed out
like yesterday's rubbish.

Father stands in the pinnace,
holds his hand to me.
"Come, Alis."
I step into the smaller boat,
less steady,
less sturdy.

Mother eases in,
cradling her belly,
perspiration at her temples,
her once-starched collar
dingy and askew.

"What will we do?" Mother whispers.
Her cheek rests on Father's shoulder.
"How will we reach the land
that's been promised us?"

"We'll find my brother and his men."

Uncle.
I grasp the wooden bird
in my pocket.
I did not dream
of seeing him so soon.
Surely he and the other soldiers
will set things right,
speak sense to Ferdinando.

Maybe he has already
caught sight of the boats,
will welcome us onshore.

Alis

Before me is a place
few Englishmen have ever seen.
I lean over the bow,
try to will the pinnace faster
to trees pointing heavenward,
a flock of cranes rippling the sky.
Mother grasps my plait,
gives my hair a tug.
"Careful," she says.

The boat cuts through the water
as wind snaps our sails,
rocks us with each wave
toward land heavy with trees,
thick with darkness.
The mysterious island,

Roanoke.

Alis

The pinnace drops anchor,
and that savage, Manteo,
offers me his hand,
the Indian who came to England
with the Governor
after his first voyage here.

I shake my head,
for even though he's lived in London
and dresses as we do,
I've seen the hair as long as a woman's
he hides underneath his hat.
I will not let him touch me.

My steps are uncertain
after our ocean crossing,
and when I stumble in the sand,
I ignore Manteo's amused smile,
choose not to stand but sit and watch
the scramble of people,
the rising tide,
the pinnace already making its way
back to the ships
for the last of us.

I scan the banks for Uncle Samuel,
but he is nowhere.

Alis

The Governor bids us to follow him
across the sandy beach.
Marsh grass swishes against my skirts.

>London's crowded streets
>smelled of rot and filth.
>I'd hold my breath,
>race my friend
>down Fish Street to London Bridge.
>Neither Joan nor I ever made it
>without pulling in deep gulps of air
>as putrid as death.

Here,
damp wood mingles
with the warm sea breeze.
The forest rises up,
takes us in,
and in the woods,
scattered all around,
pink flowers,
starred yellow in their centers,
tremble with each footstep.
I pluck a jaunty bloom,
tuck it behind my ear.

Even on summer days
the London light was weak,
fighting soot and drizzling clouds.

Here,
sunlit patches
cut through highest branches,
a brilliant red bird wings above.
Her sharp notes climb up,
spiral down.

In London stray dogs roam in mangy coats
scrounging for a scrap of meat.

Here,
waves lap the shore,
crabs dance across the sand,
berry bushes reach as high
as entryways at Bishop's Gate.

What a strange and wondrous place!

KIMI

They crash through the forest.
I crouch behind trees,
watching
as they
stumble
through underbrush.

Never did I think
these strange ones would return.
Yet here they are again.

Some think
they are spirits back from the dead.
Some say
they have invisible weapons
that strike with sickness after they've gone.

Father
said they were people
like us, only
with different ways.
But how can I believe him?

Father
is dead.

Alis

Ahead,
people gather in a clearing.
We must be near the settlement
where a few soldiers
lay claim for England.

Last year,
when Uncle left us,
he promised we wouldn't long be parted.
After his time in the Queen's service,
he'd be home again.
How surprised he'll be
to learn we've come!

I want to run ahead,
clutch him in a hug,
show him how faithfully
I've kept his wooden bird.

But my legs are unsteady.
Surely Mother needs me near.
The baby we await
fatigues her so easily.
Her face is worn.
Her golden hair
tumbles loose about her shoulders,
and I lace my arm through hers,
maybe hurry her more than she would wish,

but gently,
so as not to tire her more.

Governor White and his assistants draw together.
All about us
words clash and climb
until the Governor calls for silence.
Two men break away from the Governor's side.
He says they'll go ahead,
enter the settlement through the gate.

Even though I shouldn't,
I release Mother's arm,
drop my bundle at her feet.

"Alis!" she calls,
but I pretend I cannot hear her,
for I must find Uncle.

I skirt the crowd.
A fluttering blue bird draws me—
one with plumes as lavish as a gown.
I pray it leads me to him,
my uncle,
who knows so much of wild things,
but the bird escapes me.

Somehow
I've run
far beyond the others.

Somehow
I've reached a ditch
encircling an earthen barrier—
one ring inside another,
like the moat surrounding London Wall.
It isn't hard to slip down the ditch's side,
scale the embankment within,
and I'm in the settlement—
if this place could be called that—
with homes empty,
deer wandering through open doors,
vines twisting about windows.

Two of our men walk about,
one towering over the other,
whose nose is a mountain
of lumps and bumps.
I step back from view,
stumble,
fall into a heap of ash,
the charred remains of a building.

A scream
claws at my throat.

Bleached bones
litter the ground.

Alis

My
stomach
rebels.

I clutch my skirts,
run back
to the others.

Alis

I slip into the crowd,
careful to keep near its edge,
where I won't be so easily seen.
But no one has noticed my absence,
for all are focused on Governor White.
Twice he's come to Virginia
to map the land,
paint the creatures who live here,
determine where our city would someday be.

Our Governor knows this island
better than any Englishman,
and remembering this brings relief.

We are secure
with him near.

"George Howe Sr. and Roger Bailie
have surveyed the settlement," he says.
"It has been
empty
for some
time."

"Empty?"
        someone shouts.

"What of the soldiers?"
    another says.

A woman wails.
    "Who will help us now?"

Those bones were nothing more
than seashells, I tell myself,
the remnants of a deer.

The Governor's beard is grayer
than when we first left England.
He worries his cap in his hands.
"We are unsure what has happened," he says.

The enormous man
I saw within the settlement
whispers to the Governor.
I see him stiffen.

"Mr. Howe says
there is a building
burned
to its foundation,"
Governor White says slowly,
"the
bones
of a
man."

Uncle is safe,
I think the same words over and over,
trying to unsee, unhear
this horror.

But dread surges through me.
The Governor knows nothing
more than the rest of us.

The Governor studies his daughter,
Mrs. Dare, heavy with child.
"Ferdinando's promised
to leave us the pinnace.
For now we will rebuild,
stay through the fall and winter,
and when spring comes,
we'll sail to Chesapeake
and establish the City of Ralegh."

Father's eyes are troubled.
"Someone is dead.
Does this not concern you?
And what of the other soldiers?
Surely we should search for them."

The Indian speaks.
"Perhaps my people know something.
They live on Croatoan,
not far from here."

The Governor nods his head
too vigorously.

Father presses his lips together.

I know how he thinks:
The Governor's too hasty
to claim the pinnace.
He should force Ferdinando to take us farther.
He's too quick
to trust the soldiers are elsewhere, safe.

"Mr. Howe will lead us in," Governor White says.
The other assistants step aside.
Mr. Howe,
with fingers big as sausages, points ahead.
He strides toward the village,
where Uncle
is meant to be.

The deer scatter.
The abandoned buildings
hold fast their secrets.

Alis

My thoughts fly to Mother.
I scold myself for leaving her
with two sets of things to carry
and push back through the throng
until I'm outside the village again.

The sun has brightened her cheeks;
she tries to pin her hair.
"Mother!" I shout,
and she looks to me.

"Where have you been?
And what's this on your skirt?"
She dusts my dress,
shaking her head,
ushers me to the settlement.

I touch my ear,
discover my flower is missing.
Over my shoulder,
I study the ground behind me.

In the midst of the forest,
something shifts
like a branch might in a breeze.
A shadow flits between the trees.

This is no bird.
No wind stirs the leaves.

Something
lurks
in the woods.

KIMI

~~~

Never
have there been
women or children.

The first men, they came
with tools and gifts, left
with Wanchese and Manteo
journeying to their distant world.

The second ones came
with friendship that turned bitter,
with illness,
with drought,
eating our seed corn,
beheading Father,
Wingina,
our weroance,
leader of the Roanoke.

The third ones,
so few in number,
weren't here long
before Wanchese did away with them.

I've always thought
they were a people
of only men.

KIMI

The woman
embraces one
who must be
her daughter.

How plain they are!
No copper at their ears.
I touch the pearls about my neck,
their beauty still new to me.

The girl turns her head,
her eyes,
light as the rain-rinsed sky,
search the wood.
I step back
into
darkness.

KIMI

A woman.
Her daughter.
Holding each other.

Alawa,
my sister,
what would you think
to see the English
act so tenderly?

Alis

The settlement is not remarkable—
a tiny village flanked with four earthen walls,
one with the gate,
the other three with stations,
like turrets on a castle.
Inside we find
last year's forgotten garden
and empty animal pens,
a small collection of cottages
set about an open square,
a large building used as barracks
by the soldiers sent to claim this land,
England's presence in the New World.
Beyond these buildings are
a jail,
a chapel,
the armory,
farther still the forge.

Though most structures are intact,
neglect has left its mark.
More homes must be erected
for the families here.

After a hasty service,
the bones are covered in a grave.
Men cart the scorched remains
of the burned building,

where the soldiers stored provisions.
Some of the boys hack at the vines
encircling the abandoned cottages.

In the square,
the women cluster in a knot.
"For months, the Governor
never spoke against that Ferdinando,"
pinched-lipped Mrs. Archard says.
"And we're the ones who have to pay.
The Governor should have forced him
to stop at those nearby islands
for the livestock and fruit he promised.
The Governor should have refused
to leave the ship,
insisted we sail to Chesapeake."

"But we cannot change that now," Mrs. Dare says,
and I study her rounded frame.
When will her baby join us:
before or after Mother's child comes?

"I wonder if our spiteful pilot
will let us gather all our things," Mrs. Archard says.
"Weeks it took to pack those ships.
Weeks again we'll need.
I wouldn't be a mite surprised
if he sailed away come nightfall."

Mother touches Mrs. Archard's arm.
"The Governor will make things right," Mother says,
but the woman's face loses none of its harsh angles.

She tries to comfort Mrs. Archard,
but I'm the one
who needs her reassurance.
Uncle Samuel,
Father's only brother,
has lived with us forever.
This year apart is the only one
I've ever known without him.
Where has he gone?

Only bones
were here
to greet us.

Two boys scuffle over an axe,
another carries vines that spill from his arms.
The vine boy's eyes find mine;
swift as a pickpocket,
he moves away.
I linger, observing him,
his head a mess of curls.

Everywhere I look
it's men,
women,
boys.

There is
no one
here
like me.

And Uncle,
the one
so dear to me,
has disappeared.

"Alis?" Mother calls.
She's gone ahead,
bustling toward the buildings.
No word of tenderness,
no glance that says she shares my worries.
"Please gather our things."

I reach for our bundles,
hug them to my chest so tightly,
no one can hear me cry.

Alis

We find Father bent over a fire
in the ironmonger's shed,
already working metal
salvaged from the ruins.
His hammer sings,
high and piercing,
and I run to him,
fold into him.
He drops his hammer,
pulls Mother close,
and the three of us huddle
as a flurry of activity
continues outside.

"We are here.
We are safe.
We will find Samuel," he says.

Alis

I clutch my wooden bird,
one of the three Uncle whittled
just before he left,
the second safe with Joan,
the last one his own.

Alis

"It's a bird of Virginia," Uncle said.
His hands pressed the carving into mine.
Though its wooden body is brown as a sparrow's,
I imagine sapphire wings,
a patch of rust spread above its curved white middle,
just like the painting Uncle has described.

The graceful bird,
its wings rest so daintily.
This Uncle Samuel promised me:
Birds return home
no matter how far they fly.
One set free might wander
but will eventually rejoin his flock.

At first,
I believed this was Uncle's pledge
to return to me,
but when Father said we too
would go to Virginia,
I thought of this:

> What if a flight of birds
> followed the wandering one,
> joining him on a journey
> entirely new?

Since setting sail
my secret wish has been
that Uncle's joy
would be so great,
he'd forget England
when his service was done.
Instead he'd make his home Virginia,
fly
to the City of Ralegh,
to us,
his family.

KIMI

The whispers among my people began
the first time the English came.
They grew to angered shouts:

The English have great power,
mightier than we have seen
in the agile deer,
the arrows of our enemies,
the angry hurricane.
Able to blot out the sun.

KIMI

I run the well-worn path
beyond the stalks of beans and corn,
through the slender poles of the palisade,
past the longhouses
to Wanchese.

"There are women and children!" I say.
I have interrupted Wanchese and his men,
their shoulders baring
four inked arrows,
the marks of my father.

Wanchese shifts,
the copper beads of his necklace
burning in the sun.
"They are no worry to you.
Find your mother."

I ignore the men's impatient faces.
I should join the women in the fields.
But I remain where I am. Wanchese must understand.
"This time they've brought their families.
The English want to stay."

He springs to his feet.
"Find your mother, Kimi."

I race toward the fields,
my legs quivering at my boldness
before Wanchese.
Of all the Roanoke,
he knows the customs of the English best.
He lived in their land with Manteo
after the first ones came.

But even he
cannot know everything.

KIMI

My people,
we have been
small in number,
and the tasks
of weaving mats
and pounding corn
have come to me.

The extra work
does not burden.
I am pleased
to prepare food
if what I do strengthens us.
I am proud
my fingers bleed
if my weaving shows our skill.
I am willing
to work
if labor means
my heart will for an instant
forget Alawa,
my sister,
who should be near me.

Instead
her bones rest
with our ancestors
because of English men.

KIMI

My mother and my aunts
work side by side,
their backs bent
as they tend the crops.

Like the corn,
a woman
spreads her roots wide,
like the bean,
a woman
settles her roots deep.

The English plans have been made plain:
Women mean they'll stay.

If we hope to rid ourselves of them,
push them from us
once and for all,
we must do it
before their roots take hold.

Alis

Saws bite through wood
and hammers pound broken boards—
quick work for just our second day onshore.
The settlement buzzes with enterprise
like the streets of London on market day.

A perfect chance for me to steal away.

Alis

It is not difficult to climb the wall,
slip through the ditch unseen
to the outside world.

I must touch, hear, taste, breathe
this place that is not London,
so open and free.

Beyond the protection of the village,
the memory of the bones comes,
and I crouch low,
like a dog kicked from its shelter.

How did he die?
Where have the other soldiers gone?
Are we in danger staying here?

My damp hands wring and twist
the fabric of my dress.

Every bush,
tree,
shadowed covering
I study,
until I trust I am alone.

Only then do I
slowly stand,
let myself step
into the beauty
that beckons me.

Alis

If Uncle were with me,
we'd wander the forest;
he'd tell me the names of
the creatures we'd see.
For the unknown ones,
he'd invent new words,
speak of their habits,
their patterns,
their breed.

Some stories he'd tell me
would be filled with wonders—
three-legged horses,
birds with no wings.
I'd solemnly listen,
list hundreds of questions.
Never he'd tire
of teaching me things.

Uncle Samuel,
how I miss you.
I want to see you again.

KIMI

From my earliest days,
I knew my father as
our wise counselor,
great leader.

But Wingina belonged
to my people,
not to me.

It was Wanchese
who told me stories,
held me when storms raged,
my uncle
more attentive
than any father.

Now
Wingina
is gone.
Wanchese
is weroance.

And I am
no longer
welcomed
to his side.

KIMI

As I work
in the fields
I think of yesterday:
the English,
the women,
how Wanchese wouldn't listen.

Once I've bathed,
I escape to the woods,
where all is familiar,
where I'll be welcomed always.

I do not expect
to find
her
there.

KIMI

Hunched over the forest floor,
the girl pulls up flowers,
blind to my approach.

Alis

All is fresh here,
undisturbed by the noises of the village.
In these woods
sunlight breaks through branches,
illuminating flowers,
those star-centered beauties.
How Mother would enjoy a bit of brightness!
The stems snap easily as I pick them.

KIMI

~~~

I watch her huddled
like a fawn, unaware of danger.
She's careless in her work;
petals,
leaves
litter her feet.
She's careless in her safety
all alone.
I shift to make my presence known.

Alis

So intent am I,
I miss the girl
until she is beside me.

KIMI

~~~

Her eyes fly to me,
grow wide
but do not falter,
though she wears panic on her face.

Her skin too delicate,
like a thin-barked tree;
her body bundled,
thick like a caterpillar.

Alis

Motionless
she stands.
Markings spiral up her arms,
snake down below her fringed skirt—
the only clothing she wears—
like fine embroidery stitched into skin.
Copper flashes at her earlobes,
a rope of pearls encircles her neck.
Short hair covers her forehead,
the rest gathered behind.
She studies me.

Her gaze never wavers.

What if there are
    others hiding, waiting
        like that shadow in the woods?

A cry escapes my lips.
I turn and flee.

KIMI

~~~

Something happens
before she runs,
bearlike,
back to her people.
Something falls from her clothing,
this little wooden bird,
a nestling, resting
in my cupped palm.

KIMI

Yesterday,
I stayed hidden, watched
the girl and her mother.
Today,
I wanted her to see me.

I caught her unaware,
exposed her fear,

showed my courage,
the power of the Roanoke.

KIMI

The earth, the skies, the seas
swirl with montoac,
the power that both
shelters life and destroys.

I grasp
a piece of her strength
in my hand.

Alis

I am safe now,
yet my mind buzzes
with memories of the silent girl:
the inked marks covering her limbs,
jewelry worn on her bare chest.

I reach for Uncle's bird,
a bit of comfort.
But it's no longer in my pocket.
Not near my feet,
nor along the village path.
I twist my apron in my fist.

It is nowhere.

Alis

My bird.
It was all I had of Samuel.

The sun slants through our window
as Mother and I lay the table.
Mother's movements are slower now.
Soon our little one will come.
But even thoughts of the baby
do not excite me.

"Alis, what ails you?" Mother asks.
How can I speak,
knowing Uncle's token is missing,
remembering the savage girl?

"I'm weary," I say,
hoping she'll not inquire further.
"Then it's early to bed for you," she says.

KIMI

Above me as I walk,
two iacháwanes flutter,
their blue wings flashing
in the evening sun.
They scold and bicker
as they dip and swirl,
light on a branch,
bob like leaves racing down a river.

How happy they are,
their round white bellies
satisfied with berries,
their heads cocked
to catch each sound.
Then
with joy,
they take wing,
travel on their way.

Such gladness they share.
I've known nothing like it
since Alawa
was beside me.

Alis

After breakfast,
Mother opens our shutters
to the morning.
Mrs. Dare sweeps dust
from her open door.

"Elyoner," Mother calls.

Mrs. Dare stops her broom and steps outside,
shields her eyes from the brightness.

"I meant to tell you sooner.
My Alis is twelve, old enough
to mind your little one as well as mine."

I thump the mixing bowl
firmly on the table,
scowl at her back,
but Mother doesn't turn.
Our third day in Virginia,
and I'm already a nursemaid.

"I've told Mrs. Viccars and Mrs. Archard the same.

As they organize provisions
once they're brought ashore,
Alis can watch the boys.
Practice for our babies," she says.
I hear the smile she surely wears.

Those two creatures
I couldn't escape on our voyage here?
All they do is tug at things they shouldn't,
make messes where they don't belong.

"It will be easier for us
to cook for all the men,"
she tells Mrs. Dare.
"We'll be freer
to tend the laundry."

"Mother," I say,
"I need some air,"
and skip outside
before she can stop me.

If I'm to play nursemaid,
I won't begin this morning.

Alis

Those weeks crossing,
belowdecks in the musty hold,
I learned
that of 117 journeying to Virginia
in three vessels,
I
was the
only
girl.

Twelve wives dared join their husbands;
many more stayed behind,
waiting for life to be easier in this new world.
Five brave women traveled alone.

Of the three ships,
the women and their families sailed together,
and I was stuck with young Tommy and Ambrose.
On another ship,
the seven older boys traveled freely with their fathers,
surely joking and frolicking all the day,
becoming fast friends,
while I had
no one.

With so many new faces,
I first kept track of noses—
pointed, bulbous, hooked, and pockmarked—
more so than names.

Before setting sail,
most of us were strangers,
but after months crammed together,
I knew who bickered with her husband,
which little one ignored his father's warnings,
that old Mr. Bailie,
with the lumpy, bumpy nose,
broke wind after mealtimes.

Though Mother held me
when the waves thrashed the ship
and Father's stories helped me to escape
the stink and dark and loneliness,
I still longed for Joan in London,
remembered her expression
when we last saw each other,
the tears on her cheeks.

I miss you, Joan.
I'm so lonely
for a friend.

Alis

It is good fortune to be part of a family here,
for those with children have settled in cottages.
The rest reside in barracks.

As one of the Governor's assistants,
Father has secured
a home bordering the square.

Some say the village is a rude establishment:
There are no pipes and fountains
as there are in London,
just water from a stream.
No fish and vegetables appear in market stalls,
just those we trap in swirling waters,
those coaxed from the withered garden.

But I'll take a bit of extra work
for the forest's wild beauty,
the open skies as fair trade
for the luxuries we've left behind.

I walk as fast as is proper through the settlement,
careful not to draw attention.
Everyone is busy with his own tasks
except the boy who gathered vines.

Alis

Suddenly,
he is next to me,
briskly moving.
I will not address him,
unless he's the first to speak.

"I saw her, too."
His words are so surprising,
they mean nothing,
like those fluttering noises
Frenchmen make.

He stops.
His brown eyes pierce mine.
"The girl
in the forest
the day
we arrived."

The shadow?
Was it the same
half-naked girl?

Did he also see me yesterday
as I picked flowers,
the girl nearby?

Her approach
was as silent as
the figure in the woods.

I never asked permission
to leave the settlement,
and if he was to tell
of my wandering—

"How do you know what I did and didn't see?"
My voice pounds like Father's hammer.
The shadow was the girl.
It had to be.

The boy says nothing.

I twist the edge of my apron
about my finger.
The girl,
and now this freckled boy.
Twice now
I've been caught
unaware.

My feet quicken;
he matches each step.

"I'm George," he says.

I turn to him.
He is meddlesome,
impolite.

"How old are you, George?"

"Eleven," he says.

His face is friendly.
So close to my own age.
Just as I'd longed for
all those months at sea.

But still I'm guarded.
"I know naught of a girl," I say,
as I wonder where she might be.

George shrugs,
kicks at a shell
as he turns away.

I climb the embankment only
when I'm sure he's gone.

Alis

It is magic
here,
the trees arched above,
the sun-dappled earth below.
I want to run my hands over roughened bark,
feel the crush of leaves underfoot,
breathe deep the rich fragrance of living things.
How Uncle must have loved this forest.

Alone,
I wander,
at home
with velvet mosses,
beetles scuttling over decayed logs,
the sounds of a merry stream.

KIMI

I dance her wooden bird
across my fingertips,
perch it on the back of my hand.

The girl is not welcome here.

Her hair,
so colorless,
her eyes,
pale pools of water.

I imagine her
cowering in her village
without her power.
I want to see
her weakness.

She comes
from brutal people,
yet is as loving
with her mother as we are.

Can both things be true?

KIMI

The bird leads me
back to the forest,
where she picked the flowers,
dropped them,
and ran.

I move through the trees,
leaves soft against my feet,
near the place I saw her.

And stop.

For she is there.

Without her protection

she stands before me,

brave.

Alis

She comes,
as if she searches for me.

My thoughts jump
from tree to tree,
imagining all the spaces
an Indian might hide.

KIMI

Alis

Her hair falls to her shoulders,
like drifts of sand.

The hair at her forehead
is like a raven's wing.

With so many coverings,
the heat must oppress.

There is no shame
in her nakedness.

Why is she unadorned?

Her jewelry is magnificent.

Though my heart quickens,
I step closer.

I'm drawn
toward her.

Closer.

Closer.

Nearer.

I could

touch her.

Face-to-face.

KIMI
~~~

She is no different
without her montoac,
the same faded creature
who this time doesn't run.
Somehow she has
held on to her strength.

Alis
___

We are the same height,
the only trait we share.

Anger lunges in me like a snake:
Her people killed Wingina.
Her people put Alawa in the grave.

She stands with shoulders back.

She has come
where she's not welcome.

So curious she is to me.
Her features like a stone.

Her people
have wounded mine.
I do not hide my rage.
"You have brought us sorrow."

She uses a garbled language.
Her sounds gnash and bite.
What terror is she speaking?
How fearsome she's become!

She doesn't understand,
but her face says
I have frightened her,
made her feel my pain.

Like the planting time
follows
the hunting season,
balance
has been
restored.

Alis

Her angry sounds,
I cannot make sense of them.
Are they meant for those in hiding,
signaling when to strike?

I cannot move fast enough,
cannot escape the feeling
of a presence right behind me.

KIMI

How quickly her strength flees!
Did she think I would harm her,
a girl, alone?

I walk to the stream,
stoop to cleanse my feet,
wash off her strangeness
as an outsider does
before entering the village.

Yet I am not the stranger here.
How is it I'm behaving
as though I were the different one?

KIMI

Mother's fingers
stop their weaving.
"You've left your work undone."

She does not ask
where I have been.
Her silence
fills the space
between us.

Alis

I return to the village,
and in my haste,
slam into a figure,
land firmly on the ground.

A hand reaches for me.
I scramble back like a crab.
"Forgive me, Miss Harvie.
I did not see you."
Like hers,
his words hold rolling sounds,
their pacing unfamiliar.
Manteo.

Since our arrival,
he's kept his head uncovered,
his long hair like a horse's mane.
Above each ear his head is bald,
and he means for it to be this way.
How odd it seems
with his fine clothing,
as peculiar as
the island's wind-tossed reeds.
But not displeasing.

This time,
when he holds his hand to me,
I let him help me to my feet.

Alis

"There you are!"
Mother moves as fast as she is able,
a basket of laundry held at her side.
"I've been searching everywhere."

She grabs my hand
and pulls me with her
before I can thank Manteo.

"Mrs. Archard will expect you
every morning after breakfast.
You'll care for the children
only through mid-afternoon."

I want to stomp my foot,
kick up dust
in an unbecoming way.
Much of my time
I'll be forced to give away.

Mother stops outside the Archard door.
She tugs at my wrinkled skirt,
clicks her tongue over my dirtied apron.
"I don't know where you've been—
collecting leaves,
chasing some small creature
near the armory—
but it cannot happen again.

Your help is needed here.
Do you understand?"

I nod begrudgingly.

"Good girl."
She kisses my cheek.
"Now in you go."

I knock.
The door swings open.
Mrs. Archard's words are clipped.
"You were to be here earlier."
Perhaps she always wears a scowl,
for it's the only way I've seen her.

"Keep them occupied," she says,
and slams the door behind her.

Alis

Tommy and Ambrose squabble and push.
I am hopeless as a nursemaid.

Alis

I hold the boys' hands,
lead them to the square
where they might run about,
dig with sticks,
gather shells.
As long as
Ambrose and Tommy stay occupied,
I may stretch my legs,
lean back,
lift my face to the sun.

Tommy scoops a handful of earth,
dumps it on Ambrose's head.
Both squeal with delight.
It is no bother to me.
If they come to no harm,
they may do as they like.

I think of the girl,
her wild eyes,
her peculiar manner,
that I have spoken
of her to no one.

She came to the woods
to find me.
Those words
she wanted me to hear.
What could they mean?

If Uncle were near,
I would trust him with this secret.
Not Mother,
preoccupied with the baby,
Father,
busy at the forge,
working to rebuild the village,
unloading freight from the ships.

Uncle Samuel always understood,
made time just for me.

KIMI

No good can come
from knowing her.

Before I work,
I hurry to the forest,
take her montoac
from beneath my skirts,
and leave it buried
under the leaves
heaped on the ground.

My people,
we've had too much
of the English.

I do not want
her montoac.

Alis

The older boys pass near us,
each one carrying armfuls of wood
gathered outside the village.

George grips his bundle
as the others stack theirs
in the far end of the square.
He tilts his head toward the little ones,
their dirt-streaked faces.
"Your work is easier than mine."

"How are you certain?" I say.
"You stand here resting,
while I am busy."

His grin is broken toothed.
"Busy resting in the sun."

I cannot deny this.
Though it's hotter than
I've ever known,
though the thick air can oppress,
London was all rush
from one building to the next
to escape the rain, the stench, the filth.
Never have I loved
the outside world as now.

This time I'm the one to smile.
"Do not tell," I whisper.
"I like caring for them best
when they are sleeping."

Though I do not say it,
inside me hope awakens.
Perhaps I've found a friend.

"Your secret's safe with me," he says.

KIMI

Hunting season
brought womanhood,
planting season
my ceremony.

Four mornings past
I first saw
the girl
with water eyes.

KIMI

If Alawa had lived,
she would have given
the necklace at my ceremony—
>after the pain
>of the tattooing,
>after I emerged
>a woman
she would have fastened it
around my neck,
while voices lifted in celebration.

The skin of my arms and legs
is no longer tender,
but I have changed little.
If my sister were with me,
I would speak of this,
I would tell her
though I am now a woman
I do not yet feel grown.

But she is not here.
And I stay silent.

I do not confide
in the women, who saw
their thirteenth planting seasons long ago,
the small ones, who play
about the corn.

Mother has her sisters.
Wanchese has his men.
With Alawa gone,
there is no one else like me.
I have no one.

KIMI

The wooden bird.
I've stayed far from the place I left it,
and yet it calls,
as though it were a living thing.

All day I listen to it,
first in the fields,
while at the stream,
later as I pound the corn,
after an evening bowl of fish,
its music hasn't ended.

It says
come back for me.

I will not.

KIMI

My sleep is restless.
Darkness stretches too long.
The sun is slow to trace the heavens.

When at last
morning comes,
I put my mind
to working in the fields.

Yet I cannot escape.
The bird still calls to me.

I work until
my nails are ragged.
Dirt cakes my hands.
Mother motions to me,
gives me a sip of water.
She holds a hand to my cheek,
cool and gentle.

"Kimi, are you well?"

"Yes," I say.
But I do not believe it,
and neither does she.

"Bathe early," she tells me.
"Rest until mealtime."

I lie back in the water.
Currents swirl my hair about me.
Above, the sun journeys
closer to the earth.

Last time I saw the girl
I did what was needed,
told her
the English don't belong.
Why then does her bird
still beckon me?

If I claim it,
do I betray Wingina?
If I keep it,
do I forget Alawa?

The sun escapes the sky,
and the moon settles in its place.
I go,
kneel beside the mound of leaves,
brush away their covering.

Again the bird is
tucked in the folds of my skirt.

It has grown silent
at last.

KIMI

Those about me sleep
in the stillness of the longhouse.
My thoughts are full awake.

I clasp the wooden bird,
run my thumb over its head.
Under its chin
its feathers are roughened,
its belly smooth.
Now that it is near,
it has not made a sound.

I do not understand its montoac,
but this is clear to me:
I was never meant to leave the bird.
It is the girl's,
but somehow I, too, am joined to it.
The silence speaks this plainly.

Alis

Five days I've stayed back from the forest.
I've been busy with the children,
unsure what to make of the Indian girl.

Now the boys are with their mothers.
The afternoon is mine.
Enchantment pulls me deeper
through scattered branches,
beyond the slender saplings,
this chance to wander on my own,
discover nature's secrets
I've only known
through Uncle, when he spoke
of the Governor's paintings.

Now I can live this wild world.

Farther in,
I make my way,
don't let myself admit
exactly where I'm heading
until I'm here,
the place I've met her twice before.

What is it like
to make a home
in such surroundings?
To be born
to this wonder?

She knows.

Alis

I can't believe
she's here,
waiting for me.

This time I will show her
I am just as brave
as she is.
If she speaks,
I will not run,
but listen,
make meaning
from her sounds.

Without thinking,
I lift my hand—
a foolish gesture—
such greetings
are for friends,
not strangers,
and even so,
she wouldn't understand.

KIMI
~~~

She raises
her hand
at my approach.
There is kindness in it.
This is how
she speaks
to me.

KIMI
~~~

The Englishmen
in Wingina's time
started as our friends.

Now we are enemies.

But the girl has
not chosen
to stay away
and neither
have I.

Alis

I could not imagine going about
with my chest bare.
Never would I allow
others to ink my arms and legs.

Yet she is beautiful.

KIMI

I would not wander unaware
as she does, unprotected,
loud and stumbling
through a forest
she doesn't know.

Yet she is daring.

Alis

I stay
long enough to study
the patterns on her arms,
close enough
to meet her eyes
with no urge to lower my gaze.

We are not together,
but neither are we apart.

Three times
I have come here.
Three times
we have met.

Something
fascinating, fragile
grows between us.

KIMI

Alis

Her bird rests
in the folds of my skirt.
It has called her.
It has led me here.

I inch my hand forward,
let it hover over
the inky band about her arm.

She reaches near,
reminds me how Alawa,
entranced with a lizard,
longed to grasp
his glistening blue tail.

I touch the lacy pattern.

She presses a finger to my arm,
pulls her hand back quickly.
Her eyes rush to mine.

Did I expect her skin
to feel like wood or stone?
It is as any person's would be.

Suddenly, I smile.

I begin to laugh.

Alis

I pass into the settlement unnoticed.
Where there was activity,
now no one is about.

My insides grow cold and heavy.
I am desperate to find my family.

I stumble over abandoned tools,
skirt a basket of laundry and an overturned bench.
Everyone's assembled in the square.

To one side,
bald Mr. Pratt holds George,
who hangs like a marionette
with severed strings.

I push into the crowd.
Several women step back,
their faces covered.
I shove into the center,
where Father,
Mr. Dare,
Governor White,
Mr. Archard
hold the limbs of a man

whose back
    is riddled with arrows,
whose head
    is smashed in.

"Away, Alis!" Father says.
Tears etch his weathered cheeks.
I stagger out of the circle
past George
now crumpled on the ground,
and retch,
body heaving,
my hands pressed to my knees.

Above the clamor the Governor speaks.
"We found Mr. Howe near the shore,"
his voice breaks,
"as you see him."

The bones
the arrows
fifteen missing men—
I retch again—

Dear Uncle Samuel!
What awful things
happened here
before we came?

What
is
this
place?

KIMI

Not long after I return,
Wanchese and his men come.
They've slain an Englishman
wandering alone,
hunting crabs with a clumsy weapon.

The English have again been shown
the might of the Roanoke,
they have again been reminded
of the wrong in beheading our weroance,
in unleashing disease and crippling our people.

In the season of the highest sun,
after those that survived Wanchese's fire
broke free and fled,
my people celebrated.
Never again would we face
the betrayal of the English.

Yet here they are
with families,
and Manteo,
who never returned to the Croatoan,
but claimed the English as his own.

None is welcome here.

But there is a girl among them
I would have never known
if they had not come again.
One whose curiosity
reminds me of my sister,
one I long to understand.

Alis

The next morning I awake.
My head pounds with remembrance:
the crowd gathered in horror
around Mr. Howe.
Just one week here,
and one of us is dead,

attacked,
while I was with the girl.
He at the shoreline,
we in the woods,
was it luck he was the one
discovered?

Did she know
what was planned?
Out there,
was I in as much danger
as a murdered man?

None of us has done wrong,
yet we fear for our lives.

Alis

Mother hands me a crust of bread,
though it's not enough to satisfy.
What little food we have must last
as long as we can make it.

I shuffle to Mr. Viccars's house
to collect young Ambrose.
He clings to my sleeve
as I greet Mrs. Archard at her door.
"Remember,
they're not to dump dirt on their heads," she says,
her sharp eyes narrowed.

"It won't happen again."
I doubt Mrs. Archard
has ever had a bit of fun.

All the day
I roll a rag ball,
wipe dripping noses,
keep hands from the fire,
fetch back Tommy
when he wanders too close to the water pail,
teach them what Joan and I used to sing:

> Summer is a-coming in
> Loudly sing cuckoo
> Groweth seed and bloweth mead

and springs the wood anew
   Sing cuckoo!

It almost helps me to forget
that just this morning
the Governor and several of his men
sailed to the island Croatoan
in search of answers.

Manteo's mother,
leader of the Croatoan,
will help us, the Governor says.
He'll find the missing soldiers,
bring them back to Roanoke.

I roll the rag ball
for the hundredth time.

How can the Governor be sure of anything?

Alis

I leave the children with their mothers.
George carries a bucket of water
across the square.
The skin under his eyes is smudged,
as though last night
withheld from him its rest.

We walk together,
silent.
I don't know how
to speak of yesterday,
but I must say something.

"Which is yours?" I ask,
when we reach the cottages
on the other side.

"We lived there."
George points to a home
three doors down.
"But I'll be in the barracks now."

His words
hint at the awful way
his life has changed.
I cannot help myself.
"It's not the same
as losing your father,
but my uncle's missing."

His eyes shine with tears.
Abruptly he turns from me.
Water sloshes from the pail's edge,
drenching my feet.

Like the water,
this truth washes over me:
Mr. Howe is gone forever.
Perhaps my uncle won't be found.

Alis

The men arrive back in the village
when the sun burns low.
Manteo's tribe has promised
to tell the Roanoke we mean no harm.
The Croatoan will invite them
to talk peace with our men
ten days from now.

"To restore the friendship we once had,"
the Governor says.

What sort of friend
slays an innocent man,
I wonder,
but I am comforted to know
something has been done.

"Did you hear of the soldiers?" Father asks.
"Were they with the Croatoan?"
I reach for my bird, remember it is gone.

The Governor shakes his head.

At his sides
Father's hands
curl into fists.

"My mother says they traveled north," Manteo says.

"Toward Chesapeake?"

"Yes."
His head's still bare,
and now he wears
a chain of shells about his neck—
every day more Indian.

"If we could, we'd go to them at once,"
Governor White says.
"But it would take weeks
to move the cargo to the pinnace,
take it north,
trip by trip.
By then,
summer would be too far gone
to plant and harvest.
There'd be no time to build
before cold weather settles in."

"But is it safe here?" someone asks.
"A man was murdered yesterday."

"I understand your worry," the Governor says.
"But we are trying to set things right.
I believe it's best to stay.
We'll be reunited with the missing men next spring,
once we pass the winter here."

His words cover all of us
assembled in the twilight.
It is the first mention of leaving
since we arrived a week ago,
and though Uncle's whereabouts are unclear,
I will not lose faith.

"To Virginia!" someone shouts,
"to the City of Ralegh!"
and all around
we join
in jubilee.

"How are you sure they're still alive?"
Father's words cut through the celebration.

"There is no certainty,"
the Governor admits,
"but we hold hope close.
We have no other choice."

    "Ferdinando should take us north."
    someone says.

    "Ferdinando should take us home!"
    another answers.

The Governor's face grows red.
"Do not speak of that man to me!"
He spits the words.

"Do you know why
he agreed to bring us to Virginia?
So that he might plunder
Spanish ships along the way.
Throughout our voyage
he spoke of nothing else.
It took weeks to persuade him
to wait until he'd brought us here.
Such raiding as he hoped for
risked losing our cargo,
perhaps even our lives.

Once our goods are unloaded,
Ferdinando will be gone."

"Come."
Father grabs my hand and Mother's.
His tone holds an edge.
When talk turns to the missing men,
how quickly his emotions
bend and shift like heated iron.

Alis

Father shuts the door.
His face is drawn,
his dark eyes heavy.

"Alis."
He says my name
so gently,
it frightens me.
Why does he sound as though
he offers comfort?

"Something's
wrong,"
my words come slowly,
"something's
happened."

Father nods,
his thick, dark hair,
the squared shape of his chin,
so much like Samuel's.
Mother puts her arm about me.

I steel myself to say the words.
"It's Uncle, isn't it?"

Those lurking thoughts,
the ones I've tried

and tried
to push away
come roaring back.

"Sweet Alis," Father says,
"it's time for you to understand.
Even if Samuel
wasn't killed by the Roanoke,
with a hasty departure
in foreign waters,
what is the likelihood
the soldiers reached Chesapeake,
where none had ever been?"

This can't be.
"Samuel's strong!"
I picture him,
his head thrown back,
laughter ringing forth.
So close he feels,
so vibrant.

I cling to Father,
bury my head in his chest.
"How I've wanted to keep faith," he says.
"But each day has left
more room for doubt.
Samuel's gone.
Now Howe is dead.
How can I still believe

my brother's safe?
He's lost
and I
could not
protect him."

Mother strokes my hair.
I cry until my tears are spent,
Father's jerkin damp beneath my cheek.

KIMI

The Croatoan journey to our village.
They touch their heads and chests,
clasp hands with our men.
Mother and I bring pumpkins,
bowls of fish and berries
as the weroansqua,
Manteo's mother,
speaks with Wanchese.
They say the English came to them yesterday,
have asked for peace.

A fish slips from the bowl I hold.
Wanchese scowls,
but I know he thinks as I do.

Do they not realize
that time passed long ago?

Alis

I chew a mouthful of bread,
but it is
nothing,

feel the shock of heat
from the open door,
but it is
nothing,

hear the chatter of birds
racing above,

all nothing,

for Uncle
is gone.

August 1587

KIMI

I tell Mother I harvest berries
and return with enough
that she won't suspect
I deceive her.

Two days pass
and the girl doesn't come,
my wooden bowl less full
each time I enter our village.

The attack
has taught her
to keep her distance.

I should do the same.
Turn from her now,
I tell myself.
The English only know
to take from us,
add to our sorrow.
    Our seed corn they ate,
    stealing from a future planting.
    Our families crushed with disease,
    then stripped away.

Alawa.
Wingina.
Even Uncle
they took and changed.

But I am like a moth
dancing near a flame.
Though there is danger,
I'm drawn ever closer.

The girl.
I hope she comes again.

Alis

I haven't left the settlement
since Mr. Howe was found.

Only those
collecting wood,
hunting game,
unloading cargo from the ships
may now leave through the gate.

So many worry
we're unsafe,
even here in the village.

I cannot escape the memories
of Father and the others
holding Mr. Howe's limbs,
his back riddled with arrows,

the pain
of losing Uncle Samuel.

The Roanoke are the only tribe
who live on the island as we do.
They are responsible
for my grief,
the fears that fester here.

Yet I have not forgotten the girl.

I circle the village,
go no farther.
Hemmed in,
safe and staid.

KIMI

If I could ask Wanchese
I'd say:

Why do they dress as they do?
To speak their language,
does it feel as it sounds,
like sharpened rocks on your tongue?
What makes their skin
the color of a snake's underside?
Why do the men
not keep their faces smooth
but grow hair from their cheeks?
Do they ever bathe?
For their strong odor lingers
long after they've gone.

Though they
have brought us heartache,
must all of them
be enemies?

KIMI

I go to the place
where we first met
and wait,
until the shadows lengthen,
until the sun dips low.

Before leaving,
I pick flowers,
lay them at the base of a tree.

She will come
and see them,
know I've been here.

Alis

Once,
Joan whispered
she longed to sleep amongst the clouds,
like the moon when it rests
in the sky's cupped hands.
I tried not to laugh
at her outlandish ways.

And yet,
how ordinary life is
without a bit of fancy,
without a pinch of daring
to fill our days.

Alis

I have managed not to wake my parents.
I am not needed for another hour.

At first,
I walk along the perimeter of the village
but it is not enough,
merely skirting the border.
My thoughts return
to the marsh grass trek
when we first came,
the dappled tree trunks
where the shoreline ends
at red bark stretching high.

A breeze dances around me.
I hold my damp plait from my neck.
Everything has been so still for days;
this welcome breath of air
entreats me to follow.
I could go back for just a minute,
just one small snatch of time.

Governor White's warnings,
the sun-bleached bones,
Mr. Howe's arrow-pierced body
press into my mind,
the Indians that surely lie in wait.

And Uncle,
always Uncle.

But the green world calls,
cool and inviting.
He would understand.
Uncle's bird is out there.
The only piece of him I possess
I have managed to lose.

I check
recheck
for any movement
in the guardhouse,
breathe a silent prayer,
fight against my worries,
and rush forward.

I keep
the settlement at my back,
the forest ahead.

The girl in the wood.
Will I see her again?

Alis

She is not here
amidst the branches full of fragrant needles
made richer in this sprinkling rain,
the red trunk dressed in moss,
its bark a bolder hue in dampness,

but at my feet
a wilted posy

of starflowers.

I lift them to me,
bury my face in their petals,
this offering.

It is too early.
Usually I've seen her
past mid-afternoon.

I take the ribbon from my plait,
weave it around the stems.

I will come back,
the flowers say.

Alis

I wonder what Joan would think
of the Indian girl,
how my loneliness has lessened
in knowing she is somewhere near.

KIMI

After the rain
I find them.
The flowers
still rest at the base
of the moss-covered tree.
Though storms have pounded
many petals away,
there is a red ribbon
wound about the stems.

Alawa,
my joyful sister,
danced with colored ribbons
streaming from her hands.
They were a gift from the Englishman
in Wingina's time.

This ribbon is for me.

I twist it about my fingers,
marvel at its elegance,
wish I could adorn my skirt
with its grace.

But this treasure
cannot be displayed.
I hide the ribbon
in my skirt's deerskin folds
with the wooden bird.

The girl has told me
she will come
when she is able.

I will be here,
waiting.

KIMI

Alawa,
I remember
stroking your cheek, round as a pumpkin,
pushing back your tangled hair,
your face clenched in pain.
I stayed with you,
brought the water gourd,
covered you when the cool air taunted,
promising hatred
for those who brought this illness
that was your end.

Sister,
forgive me.
I have not kept my word.

Wingina,
I see
what you first embraced.
Though their appearance is foreign,
at times in them I glimpse something familiar.
Though their montoac injures,
it is also capable of marvelous things.

Father,
I am sorry
I did not seek your wisdom.

Wanchese,
I feel
your hatred,
know you reject their ways.

Uncle,
I ask your pardon,
for I cannot think as you do.
There is one among them
I long to understand.

KIMI

Her montoac
is not a thing
for me to keep.

It is right
to return what is hers.

Alis

It has been days
since I've seen her,
yet this time when I go
she is there.
She smiles,
extends her hand to me—
cradling Uncle Samuel's bird!
Where did she find it?

I kiss it,
clasp it to my cheek,
and for a moment,
it is as though
he's with me.

Her other hand is heaped with berries.
I shove them in my mouth,
hardly chewing,
their sweet goodness
dripping off my chin.

Alis

"Alis," I say,
pointing to myself,
for after everything
that has passed between us,
it's only proper she know my name.

She touches her head,
holds a hand over her heart.
"Kimi."

Alis

This must
remain secret.

We share
no language.

Because of her tribe,
we live in fear.

Yet she's shown
me kindness.

She is Kimi,
a Roanoke Indian.

She has
become

KIMI

My people
would not understand.

She does not
know our customs.

The English
tried to destroy us.

She knows
beauty.

Alis,
an English girl.

my friend.

KIMI

So many things
I want to share,
so much I want to know.

Alis

If only
the sun would stand in place,
time might stretch
and
slow.

Alis

We point to objects,
name them
with the speech we were born into.
We trade sounds,
collect them
as Joan kept pretty buttons.

I practice Kimi's words,
strive to make the vowels dance as she does.
She follows the curving of my lips,
trains her mouth to utter noises
it never has before.

Her sounds in trying English
are like a child's babble.
When I test her phrases on my tongue,
she tugs her ear to say
I must speak just as strangely.

In this way we communicate,
a stilted mixture
of two languages,
one that's
ours alone.

KIMI

~~~

We stretch out in the sunshine,
point to the clouds skimming the trees.

"A fox," I say,
and make my hand
a sharp-nosed creature
opening his jaws.

She looks above,
holds her palms together,
weaves them like a fish
thrashing in the waters.

I see a snake,
its slender body
streams across the sky.
She finds a bird,
a puff of mist,
a gauzy veil
with outstretched wings,
that swoops and stretches
with the wind,
breaks apart and forms again.

I tug my ears,
use my eyes to tell her
to look above.

Alis sees the rabbit cloud.
She crouches,
hops,
holds back laughter
with her hand.

Alis

I have my bird.
I know her name.
The girl,
she is my friend.

It is so strange
returning to the village,
coming back to the familiar.

Perhaps this is why
I signal to George
when I see him passing.
He leaves the other boys,
a shovel in his hand.

He pushes back his dampened curls.
"I see you're hard at work again."

I wave his words away.
"I have something to tell you."
My voice drops to a whisper
as he draws closer.

"The Indian girl,
I saw her
when I was in the woods."
Saying it is such relief.
"I've told no one else."

His eyes grow round.
"You've left the village
though the Governor has forbidden it?"

Too late I realize
I should have kept my secret.

"Not recently."
I search his face to see
if he might catch me in my lie.
But all I find is sadness.

How could I forget his father,
what happened just a week ago?

"It's too dangerous out there," George says.

This place that captivates me
is where his father died.
I want to tell him
I understand his loneliness,
but the words stick in my throat.

He checks to see no one else is near.
"It is best to keep the girl between us."

Alis

Throughout the early hours,
I think of all the day might hold.

When the afternoon is mine,
I sneak away,
I rush and run,
but doubt creeps in
as I near our meeting place.

Perhaps now that my bird's returned
she will not come again.
Perhaps her happiness yesterday
was only just pretend.

Then I see her waiting—
her dark eyes bright,
a warm smile on her face.

My footsteps quicken,
until I reach her side.

Alis

"Eight days and no response
from the Indians," Father says.

Mother's head is bowed.
Her breakfast remains untouched.

"Two days are left."

"And then?" I ask.

He doesn't speak for a long while.
Deep creases cut between his brows.
"That is none of your concern, Alis."

He thinks
I'm too young to understand,
too childish to see
this mess we're in.

Alis

Later that morning,
I walk with Ambrose and Tommy past the shed,
hear the clear notes of Father's hammer.

He stops his work,
steps outside.
"How are the little ones?"

The boys settle in the dirt,
kick their legs until it swirls about them.
"Troublesome. Mischievous."

A smile grows across his sun-browned face.
He pinches my cheek.
"Similar to a girl I'm acquainted with," he says.
"How are you, my Alis?
It cannot be easy as the only girl."

It is lonely
with no one here
like me.

"I've spoken with George Howe."

I would never tell of Kimi.

"George.
I hope to train him to work with iron
alongside me in the forge.
Poor boy,
a bit of guidance is what he needs."

Alis

"Hurry, Alis," Mother says from the doorway.
Father and the other assistants
have gathered in the clearing.
We flock with others to the bonfire,
where the light overpowers
the sun's first hint of morning.

"The morrow marks ten days
since we asked for peace," the Governor says,
"with no answer from the Roanoke."

They are the only tribe
living on this island.
Surely their promise
is the one we most need.

"Have the Croatoan sided with us?" someone says.

The buttons on Manteo's doublet
flash in the firelight.
The buckles on his shoes gleam.
"My people trust the Englishmen."

Manteo's home is on a nearby island.
Father says it's easier to remain friendly
with a bit of distance between.

The Governor and his assistants form
one solemn line.
Father's eyes take in everyone,
but refuse to find me.
I cling to Mother's elbow,
wish for the Governor
to steer this meeting elsewhere,
hope the fear bubbling inside me is unfounded.

Governor White speaks:
"The Roanoke have
in their silence
asked
for
war."

The assembly shifts and murmurs,
moves like the ocean that brought us here.

Father stands with George,
the boy who has no father now.

"Tonight we go," the Governor says.

Alis

The Roanoke have caused us harm.
They have killed,
forced us to live in fear.

But there is Kimi—

Alis

She must know.
All morning I think of nothing else.

Once time's my own,
I take no care in hiding
but flee the settlement in haste.

My mind is flooded with one image:
Kimi lying in the forest,
injured and alone.

She must learn
what is planned.

"Go!" I say,
though she's not in our meeting place,
and my word is nothing to her.

I journey deeper
through the trees,
rush past brambles
that scrape my hands,
catch my sleeves.

"Go!"

Only the forest hears me,
and it keeps silent.

KIMI

I kneel by the stream.
Water flows over my hands,
loosening my tired fingers,
washing away
a day's labor
in the fields.

From behind me
there's a sound,
but I
see nothing.

Mother and her sisters
stand together,
laughing as they cup the water,
letting it run down their arms.
I watch them
crowded about Nuna,
the first baby born to us
since the English illness
killed so many.

Do English women
gather together
after work is done?

Do they form ties
with one another
that cut as deep as rivers?

If their women are like ours,
are we so different after all?

Again I hear it,
a voice
repeating
one frantic word.

Could it be Alis?
To come this close,
to risk discovery.
What would bring her so near?

Mother and her sisters are occupied,
absorbed in one another.
I slip away.

KIMI

Through the cedar grove I race.

"Go!"

The word is louder now,
comes from somewhere
near the walnut trees.

"Alis?"
My voice just a whisper.
Near my village,
no one must hear me
call to the English girl.

Alis

Doubt licks about my middle.
Kimi will not understand,
and what am I doing,
trying to warn
the very ones
who killed Mr. Howe,
took Uncle from me?

As quickly as I came,
I race back to the village
before anyone discovers I've gone.

KIMI

~~~

Far ahead,
I glimpse
a flash of blue
soon swallowed by the trees.

Alis.

I should have shouted,
shown her I was near!

KIMI

Go.

What it means
I do not know,
but there is montoac
in the sound.

KIMI
~

Rushing,
I enter my village.
"Wanchese!" I shout,
where he and his men assemble.

This time
I need
no permission
to approach our leader,
for Wanchese
must listen.

He rises,
arms crossed,
peers down at me.

"Go," I say.
I do not know the word,
but my uncle does.

"Where did you hear this?" he asks.

"Go," I say again.

Wanchese takes my hand
as he did when I was younger.
"Why do you say
this English word to me?"

"I heard it."
I must be careful,
guard what I tell him.

"Where?"

"In the forest."

His roughened fingers
remind me how I miss him.
In this moment,
he is not weroance,
but simply Uncle.
"What does it mean?"

"It means to leave,"
Wanchese tells me.
"Move away."

He drops my hand,
lifts my chin with his fingers.
"Have you seen the English again?"

I do not deny this.
There is no need
to tell him more.

Wanchese rests his other hand
on the quiver at his waist.
He calls to the others:

"Go to the English village
and learn what happens there."

The men scatter as ants.

He leans in close to me,
our weroance once more.
"We are not done.
We will speak of this later."

KIMI

The sun is gone.
Wanchese's men race back,
form a tight circle about him.

"Gather the women and children," Wanchese says.
"We depart for Desemunkepeuc
immediately."

KIMI

Desemunkepeuc,
our mainland village,
where all my people live together
for the hunting time.

My family is one
who dwells on this island,
where the shellfish are abundant.
They feed us
during the earing of the corn,
as we wait for crops to ripen.
We return to Desemunkepeuc after harvest.

If we go now,
we leave our corn untended,
abandon these rich waters.

"We were not prepared
when they came for Wingina,"
I hear Wanchese say.

"This time
the English
will not touch us."

Alis

I keep my own counsel,
and my silence eats away at me.

I should have tried to find her,
somehow made her understand.
But I left before she heard me.
I have failed her in this way.

Alis

The cottage is empty
with Father gone.

Sleep is slow in coming,
like the night Uncle told us
he would sail to Virginia.
He went to serve his Queen,
but the Governor's watercolor paintings
are what truly led him here.

That night,
Mother pressed her cheek to mine,
returned to her mending.
Father told me to dry my tears.
It was Uncle
who sat nearby,
held my hand,
whispered of strange and glorious creatures
until dreams found me.

Now
it is only in my dreams
Uncle holds me close.

Alis

Before day breaks
the men stumble back,
eyes like embers,
knees muddied.
George is the last to enter,
a too-big musket
strapped across
his narrow back.

Governor White
holds his head
in his hands.
"How could I know?" he says
over,
and over,
until Ananias Dare
leads him away.

"What has happened?" Miss Lawrence asks.
No one answers.
The men
disappear in the darkness.

If there had been victory,
they would have stood solid,
told of their valor.
If there had been defeat,
some would be missing.

What could be wrong?
A few women follow their husbands,
but most stay,
a sturdy semicircle
wanting more.

Manteo is the only one to remain,
his words louder than I've ever heard before:

"We ambushed the camp."
He stops,
shuts his eyes for a moment.
"But the Roanoke were gone.

My people
were there
instead."

I cannot help but gasp.
Mrs. Archard glares,
young Miss Lawrence puts a finger to her lips.
I pay no notice.
Kimi's people were gone!
She is somewhere safe.
But why were the Croatoan
at the Roanoke village?

I fade into the crowd,
search for George.
Surely he knows more.

I find him near the empty animal pens,
alone,
his shoulders hunched,
the musket still across his back.
My footsteps slow.
Things were strange
last time we spoke.
His father's death,
the lie I told,
how carelessly I spoke of Kimi.
But I must know
what happened.

"George?"

He lifts his head.

"Tell me," I say.

Alis

"We crept to the village,
started firing."
George's face is vacant,
empty as a broken promise.
"The Indians scattered,
seeking cover in the reeds.
The darkness filled with voices
shouting Manteo's name.
Even I understood their pleading.

"When he recognized his tribe,
Manteo fell to his knees.
But it was too late.
Several already lay dead."

I try to imagine
what it was like for Manteo:
Attacking our foes,
finding family instead.

"The Roanoke
had abandoned their camp.

The Croatoan told us they'd come as promised,
left their island early, so as not to miss
the opportunity to talk peace.
When they discovered the empty village,
they stayed to gather the corn
the Roanoke had left in their haste."

George's head falls back
against a fencepost.
"And so,
we attacked
our friends."

Alis

"Alis!"
Father calls to me.

"I must go," I say.

George doesn't answer,
just stays as he is,
staring into nothingness.

"Alis!"
Father's voice is a fire,
his white shirt soiled and untucked.
"Where have you been?
I could not find you."

He pulls me with him.
I try to match my stride with his,
but I cannot keep pace.

"The Governor holds out hope
the Croatoan will forgive us,
but I cannot believe it.
We have two enemies now."

Father doesn't release my arm until our door,
where Mother busies herself with sweeping.
"Stay with your mother when you are outside."

Cold rushes over me.
Outside, he says.
Surely Father doesn't know
I leave the settlement.
"What do you mean?"

"Stay near to her!
What more must I say?"

"Alis."
Mother sings my name,
a warning to take care.
Eager to make peace,
she reaches for Father's hand,
places it in mine.
"Alis cannot always be with me.
She cares for the little ones
while I cook and launder,
goes home when she is done."

Guilt stabs me.
Many days
I roam
outside
the village walls.

"We've made quick enemies," Father says.
No one is safe."

"Dyonis, our daughter will not be unwise."
Mother turns to me,
her eyebrows raised,
looking for my confirmation.

I nod,
but I cannot hold her gaze.
My mother's trust
is nothing I deserve.

Her mouth's turned down,
her forehead creased.
"If you are careful,
if you promise
to hurry home each day,
I must believe
you will be safe."

Father slumps into a chair,
covers his face with his hands.
"Samuel."

"There is nothing
you could have done
to save him," Mother whispers.

Grief floods me again.
Will this heartache ever lessen?

The dangers
Father speaks of,
how far we are from safety,
the hurt with Uncle gone.
All this, yet I am certain:

Even threats of peril
will not keep me from my friend.

Alis

All day the men cut slender trees,
form wooden poles
sunk in the ground inches apart.
Outside the earthen wall and ditch,
they are a third ring of protection
to secure the village border.

The poles are partly fence,
partly cage.
Father calls it a palisade,
made in the manner of the Indians.

One more barrier
to hold back danger
and keep us apart.

KIMI

Word comes of what happened
in our village yesterday,
how the English
attacked their friends,
ones they'd earlier begged for peace.
How Manteo himself,
so hungry for their montoac,
so changed by their customs,
didn't recognize his own
until it was too late.

If,
like Wanchese,
he'd returned to live with his people
and rejected the English,
disgrace wouldn't mark him
as it does now.

KIMI

What haste.
What cruelty.
The English
attack without first knowing
whose children they destroy.

Alongside my cousins
who always live in our mainland village,
I work the fields,
yanking at weeds so roughly,
a bean plant loses its fragile hold.

I remember Alis,
her bravery
in warning me.

More gently now,
I pat the soil around the bean,
trace its growth from roots
to spindly stalk interwoven with the corn.

These two plants thrive together,
make my people strong.
There is no reason to let my anger
uproot something good.

Alis

For days,
we rush through open spaces,
mark the distance
from door to door.
Surely the Croatoan steal about the edge of camp;
the Roanoke prowl in the woods.

Alis

Though it's not Sunday,
all work is left undone.
In the open square we congregate
for Manteo's baptism.

Today he'll officially become
a servant of the Queen.
Once we've left to begin our city,
he'll be the one who
will stand for England,
will represent our nation here.

Voices whisper all around me,
wondering at the Governor's hurry.
Some think he hopes
two leaders will ease fears.
Others say he wants to prove
Manteo's on our side.

Governor White stands,
holds the Book of Common Prayer.

O LORD God of hosts, most loving and merciful Father,

Do I imagine hesitation
as Manteo kneels
and the Governor rests a palm
on his dark hair?

We most humbly beseech thee to save and defend Manteo, Lord
of the Island Roanoke, and thy servant Elizabeth, our Queen.

Together,
we bow our heads.
Though it is only morning,
the sun already blazes
across my shoulders.

O heavenly Father, the practices of our enemies are known
unto thee. Turn them, O Lord, if it be thy blessed will, or
overthrow and confound them for thy name's sake.

I think
of Kimi,
my new friend,

Suffer them not to prevail.

Mr. Howe,
his body battered,

Permit not the ungodly to triumph over us.

We have not obeyed thy word: We have had it in mouth, but
not in heart; in outward appearance, but not in deed.

We have lived carelessly.

the ambush on the Croatoan,

We have deserved utter destruction.

the way we've been abandoned to this place.

But thou, Lord, art merciful, and ready to forgive. Therefore
we come to thy throne of grace, confessing thee to be our only
refuge in all times of peril.

How strange to know an Indian
is the Queen's own man.
Governor White says
this has always been the plan,
to bestow him with this title
for his faithful service.
Yet
I cannot forget
the awful mistake
made four days past.

Does Governor White
also give this honor
to atone for the attack?

Manteo,
what causes you to stay?
What truly holds you to us?

KIMI

~~~

The sun is a burning fire,
makes my work
unbearable
in its unforgiving heat.

I sit,
thankful for the water gourd,
and wipe the sweat and dirt
from my face.

"Kimi."

The young ones who play
among the corn and beans
go still,
silent.

Wanchese has come to the fields
where men only enter
to help the women
break up ground
before the planting time.

Uncle has come for me.

KIMI

We rest together
in the shade of cedars.
I can almost pretend
things are
as they were
when I was younger,
that Wanchese
is only here to speak
of the teeming fish
he's trapped in the weir,
the new canoe
he hollows.

But things
are different
now.

"You must tell me
how you learned
that word," Wanchese says.

Four days
I've dreaded this,
have had no way
to answer him
that would not lead to lies.
I grasp a stick,

swirl patterns
on the ground.

"What is it, Kimi?"

I have no one, Uncle.
An English girl
has shown me
how lonely I have been.

But I cannot tell him.

The silence grows uncomfortable,
but I will not fill it.
I continue with my drawings,
loops and lines and circles.
Uncle brought me here.
He should be the one to speak.

He stills my hand.
Finally I look to him.

"It's not yet time to harvest.
The mainland stores are almost gone.
We've become a burden
with so many here to feed.
We leave tomorrow."
He stands.

"Stay away from the English village.
Go nowhere near them.
Do not let your curiosity
risk our safety."

Uncle,
I want to say,
I've brought no harm,
but our security.

Alis

News comes hours later
from those at the beach.
Mr. Florrie rushes from door to door,
his wild hair on end,
telling all to stay inside.
Indians came ashore,
surrounded those unloading cargo,
grotesque paint covering their bodies.

His escape is a miracle!

Is Mother safe with the other women?
Has Father left to help the men?
The boys fret to go outside.
I distract them with songs,
by counting fingers, knees, and noses.
They cry for their mothers.
How I want mine also,
but I must be the one to comfort.

An hour passes, more,
before the men return
and it is safe to leave the cottage.

It was the Croatoan,
Manteo's people.
They were poised to attack,
but Manteo persuaded them

to put down their weapons,
promised our friendship once again.
How I hope
our fragile bond
has been renewed.

Mother rushes to me,
cups my cheek in her hand.
"My Alis."
Like the little ones,
I cling to her, so grateful we are safe.

Alis

We are all of us
still shaken,
though the present danger's passed.
"Hurry home," Mother tells me.
"Stay close to the buildings."

Around me,
shadows reach like snakes,
deepen into darkness.
I clutch my cloak,
though the evening stifles without a breath of air.
It is then I see George,
striding like a soldier toward a cluster of boys,
which grows tighter as he enters.

George swings a musket over his shoulder,
marches in place with his chest out,
the picture of a fighting man.
He boasts about the ambush
and his bravery that night,
brags he would have shot a Croatoan
at the shore today.

The others cheer him on.

To see him act like this,
to hear him speak as though
he enjoyed the fight,
it is like the shock of cold metal
held against my skin.

KIMI

We pole our boats
until the land falls away
and all around is endless ocean,
the early morning sun.

Paddles pull
as the dugouts
cut the waters,
where one thrashing wave
could overcome us,
wash us to the dark world
swirling below.

Beside me, Mother stops,
stays focused on the shore.
"Remember how Alawa danced?"

My sister's name stirs images
of her twirling with the ribbon,
running through the lapping currents,
so alive to wonder.

For the first time since
my little sister's death,
her memory brings
no stabbing pain.

KIMI

At our island home,
men and women flock
to the roaring fire.
Wanchese weaves and bows,
the gourd rattle dancing with him.
Others spin like eagles soaring,
arms held wide,
heads to the heavens,
making merry.

Songs rise in thanksgiving,
a cry to appease destruction,
restore the fragile balance of the living,
a ceremony marking our return.

Alis

"Do you hear that?"
Father leans against the doorframe.
"How can I not?" Mother's forehead wrinkles.
"Those awful sounds."

The pounding
is close enough
to challenge my own heartbeat.
The chants
climb and fall in eerie wails.
Kimi's tribe has returned.

"Manteo vows it's a ritual
to celebrate their safety," Father says.
"But it sounds as though
the Roanoke
prepare
for attack."

"Manteo."
Mother frowns.
"They say yesterday
he persuaded his tribe to turn back,
but I find it hard to trust him."

KIMI

How good it is to be here,
in these fields I know best,

How right to be near Alis
once more.

Alis

There are even more men
guarding our borders now.

Will I ever
leave the settlement
again?

Alis

I awake at the first hint of morning,
slip my feet into my shoes,
am careful the door closes
softly behind me.

If there is a way
out of the village,
I will find it.

Already I have planned
what I'll say if I'm found missing.
The sunrise beckoned.
I watched it from the armory.

How easily
the lie comes to me.

The wall runs unbroken
around the settlement.
There are two guards
at each post,
eyes everywhere.

I pass from station to station,
study the men within,
and finally there's
Hooked-Nosed Mr. Cooper curled upon the floor,
his arm pillowing his head

and Old Lump-and-Bump's bulging frame
balanced on a stool,
his lips quivering as he snores.

I scale the wall,
jump over downed branches,
leap beyond gnarled roots.
I do not turn back,
do not stop
until I am in the place
where Kimi meets me.

I've never seen her
in the early hours,
but here I sit,
imagine Kimi near.

In my mind,
there are no barriers.
My words and hers
make perfect sense between us.
I ask about
her family,
tell her
what a wonder
this island is to me.
I speak of Uncle,
young enough to be a brother,
the person dearest to me,
that trusting he loved this beauty

helps ease his absence;
believing her world
is one he embraced
keeps him close to me.

My heart is satisfied
with the conversation we've shared,
even if it's only been pretend.

With my finger,
I write in the dirt—
a skill Mother and Father
never understood my wanting—
yet I am grateful
Uncle taught me this.

A-l-i-s

K-i-m-i

A steady rain begins,
washes my words away.

Something moves
behind the red-barked trees.
I leap to my feet.

An Indian,
his arrow!

He means to kill me!

So fast,
so fast
I run,
my breath
comes
raw
and
jagged.

Alis

All morning
I think of him,
his arm pulled back to let the arrow fly,
the feathers woven in his hair.

Indians are out there,
waiting to strike,
yet I only know of this
because I left the settlement.
I can say nothing
without condemning myself.

Since Mr. Florrie warned us
of the Croatoan on the shore,
I've kept Ambrose and Tommy inside for days.
A bit of sun would do them good.
I lead them to the empty square,
far from the walls.
Surely here we're safe.

They gather shells,
laugh to watch
them thud or skip
across the ground.

George marches to us,
a musket at his shoulder,
a knife tucked in his breeches.

He sits back on his heels
so he is level with the boys.

"When you're old enough
I'll teach you
to aim those at the Indians,
shoot them with a musket,
bash in their brains."

"Don't say such things!"
I press the boys against my skirts,
covering their ears.

George smirks,
his broken tooth catching his lip.
"Do you think the Croatoan
truly have forgiven us,
that the Roanoke don't know
we meant them harm?
Surely both hide in shadow
just outside the village boundaries."

My heart turns over painfully.
The man I saw this morning.
It is just as George has said.
How long will we be safe?

Days ago,
this boy wept openly.
Now he seeks a chance to strike.

I hope my words will reach the empty part of him.
"You must miss your father terribly."

For a flash he is unguarded,
then a steeliness comes over him.
"Don't speak of him again," he says.

KIMI

Tonight,
after our meal,

the drums begin,
the men approach,
gourd rattles in their hands.

"I saw a girl,"
Chogan says.
"Notched an arrow to frighten her.
She fled like a rabbit."

Cold grips me.

The men hold their rattles high.
Drums pound in unison,
lead the dancing men.

We are here,
their movements say,
have been since the earth's beginning.
It is you Englishmen
who don't belong.

Alis

Mother and Mrs. Archard have finished their work early.
The afternoon is mine to do with as I please.
"Why you choose
the heat outside
is senseless," Mother says.
She doesn't long to see everything about us,
explore all that is unknown.

But she understands this need in me.
She lets me go.

I am grateful
for what I've been offered.
Mother says I'm free to wander
if I stay near.

I stroll about the village.
I lift my eyes to each station
as I walk beside the earthen wall,
running my hand along its sturdy side.
My fingers find
part of the structure has melted
in last night's rain.

The Indian,
his arrow,
they make me hesitate.
But the pull to go to Kimi,
even stronger.

This will be my way out.

Behind me
is a guardhouse.
Before me,
a group of men pass
with boards over their shoulders,
saws in hand.

So as not to draw attention,
I walk farther on,
and once no one is about,
I hurry back,
pray the guards are focused elsewhere,
and plunge my hands
into the wall's damp softness
until I've widened
the space.

I escape.

Alis

"Good day," I say, when I see her.
Kimi clutches my hand,
touches my forehead,
my heart, with our fingers intertwined.

She slips my shoes upon her feet,
stumbles in them
like one new to walking.
I unwind my plait,
motion to her
to fashion my hair like hers.

Here
I can forget
all else,
I can pretend
this moment
is how things always are.

KIMI

Alis spins about,
arms spread wide,
so like Alawa.

All I shared with my sister,
what I've pushed away so long
stirs to life within me,
like an evening breeze,
a bee in search of nectar,
a gushing stream.

I join her dance,
the world a blur of colors,
like the leaves that float at harvest,
the memory of a dream.

Together,
we spin,
fall to the earth in laughter,
leaves clinging to our hair.

KIMI

Her question I do not follow,
but when she lifts her hand,
one finger raised,
I see the bird.
It flies from branch to branch,
as blue as the morning.
"Iacháwanes," I say.

Her lips move.
"Ia-chá . . ."

She wants the word
to be her own.
"Iacháwanes."

"Ia-chá-wa . . . ," she tries again.

". . . nes," I finish for her.

"Ia-chá-wa-nes."

The little bird bobs,
makes music in his throat.
I remember the two that flew above
the first time we met.

And then it comes to me.
Her wooden bird,

the roughness underneath his beak,
perhaps it is the copper feathers
iacháwanes wears.
I cup my hand,
stroke imaginary wings.

She doesn't follow.
I hook my thumbs together,
make my fingers fly.

Slowly Alis smiles,
pulls the wooden bird from her coverings,
holds it high enough the creatures
seem as though they perch together.
"Iacháwanes.
Uncle Samuel's bird," she says.

Tears brighten her eyes,
but it's as if she's come alive.

Is this why her bird called me,
wouldn't let me leave it hidden?
For her joy to be restored,
so I'd awake to happiness.

KIMI

There's so much risk in our meeting.
I think of Chogan,
his arrow drawn.
"Be careful, Alis," I say,
my hand upon her wrist.

She gazes at me curiously,
tucks the bird inside her coverings.
Is her montoac enough to keep her safe?

Alis

Uncle's gift to me,
I have received it threefold,
the first in his giving,
the second time from Kimi's hand,
now today in learning its true name.

I bid her farewell,
skip back toward the village,
reflecting on this perfect day.

I do not see the man
until he stands beside me.
In one sharp instant
yesterday
and the arrow
leap to memory.

Though his hair falls past his shoulders,
he wears a crimson doublet.
"Miss Harvie."
Now I can breathe.
It is only Manteo.

I reach for the leaves
that surely stick to my hair,
realize it is bound like Kimi's.

"It is dangerous for you to be here on your own."

I tug my hair loose,
plait it hastily,
secure it with my ribbon.

He steps aside to let me pass,
but as he does he whispers:
"Iacháwanes."

The skin tingles on my arms.
I do not hesitate in rushing home.

Alis

My pace has slowed,
but my heart still races.
Manteo knows I was with Kimi.
Will he tell what he has seen?

Near the shed,
Father stands with George,
whom he now trains.
"We must stay safe," Father's saying,
"leave before the spring."

I cannot pass unnoticed.
"What are you doing?" Father asks.

"Fetching water," I say,
hoping the words sound true.

"Where is your bucket?
And why are you so filthy?"

Digging at the wall
has left my hands
smeared with mud.

George studies me knowingly.

"Truly, Alis,
where is your sense?"

I have no answer,
just hasten my steps,
for I must wash,
refresh our pail
before Father arrives home.

Alis

All morning,
all afternoon,
the women bustle about
to make Mrs. Dare comfortable.
I wait near the doorway so as not to be a nuisance.
They bump me,
step around
Tommy and Ambrose playing at my feet,
until Mrs. Archard tells me sharply
to take the children from the cottage.

I skip from the doorway,
the boys' hands in mine.
Mrs. Dare's child
means my duties with these little ones
will end after today.

A baby sleeps,
cries for milk,
retires to the cradle.
My work won't be so taxing.
Perhaps, there will be time
to go to Kimi.

But I think
of George's certainty
the Indians wait to strike,
how Father talks
of leaving before spring.

KIMI

Since our return
the men
have danced each
evening,
have crafted arrows
at the fireside,
told stories
of victories past.

In this way
they prepare
for attack.

Wanchese says
the English are cruel,
hasty, undisciplined,
slaughtering all before them,
while we
wait for the perfect moment.
We fight
with precision.

I fear for what
this means
for Alis.

We
were able to go
to our mainland village.
But there is nowhere
she
can run.

Alis

Mother's scream rips me from my sleep.
"Fetch Mrs. Archard," Father says,
before he even lights a candle.

I fly to the Archard home,
bang at the door.
A slit of light grows as it opens.
"The baby!" I shout.

So long I've waited,
it is impossible to believe
today I'll truly be a sister.

Behind me,
Mrs. Archard marches,
pushes past me at our threshold,
snatches the candle from Father's hand.
Mother leans against her pillows,
tells me to leave with Father.

Through the darkness,
birds trill their morning songs,
and Father ushers me to his work shed,
where we sit by the fire,
enjoy the luxury of a bit of tea.

"I was almost a man
when my brother was born.

But when you came,
your uncle Samuel was a boy,
and he stayed forever by your side."

It warms me to think
I might be to our baby
as Uncle was to me.

Hours later,
Mrs. Archard finds us
beside the glowing coals,
her face as stern as always.
"You have a son," she says.

Alis

He is pure sweetness,
soft as dough left to rise
by the fire,
swaddled in a blanket
and in his cradle laid.

He is all sighing,
squeaking,
blinking,
a marvelous creation,
my precious brother, Samuel,
tiny babe.

KIMI
〜

Mother,
I feel
the emptiness you carry
every time you pull me close,
the ache that speaks of your missing one,
Alawa,
the longing to touch her again.

I should attend to you
as two daughters would,
yet so swiftly I deceive you
to meet my friend.

Alis

As Mrs. Dare and baby Virginia have done,
Mother and Samuel must both rest,
and since I've had a bit of bread
and Father works at the forge,
I kiss the baby's head,
encourage Mother to sleep.
I watch until their eyes flutter closed,
escape outside into the sun
to breathe deep the salty breeze.

From post to post I wander,
hoping to find a guard who's missing,
distracted from his work.

At the station near the garden,
I see Manteo within.
Our eyes meet.
He inclines his head toward the wall,
turns his back to me.

He gives me permission
to cross over?
He said it was dangerous
for me to be alone.

Out there
where a man could wait,
his arrow aimed to strike,

out there
where Kimi waits for me.

Does he signal
because he knows the way is clear?

In haste I go,
before I can change my mind,
before anyone might see.

KIMI

How she talks,
her blue eyes dancing,
holds her arms as though
cradling something dear.

A baby?
My memory revives.
Her mother was with child
when they first came.

What a gift this little one will be.

KIMI

It's always here we meet.
So much Alis hasn't seen.

"Come."
I grab her hand,
pull her with me.

We run
past thick-limbed oaks,
the beech and ash and maple trees.

I show her maquowoc
hanging from his tail,
the earth below, his sky above,
the sweet goodness of the strawberry,
at the shore,
digging down,
how cool the sand can be.

Eyes closed,
Alis smiles,
her toes burrowed deep.

Alis

What a world,
this place
Kimi's opened to me.

KIMI

We sit together,
content with silence,
satisfied
in knowing the other's near.

Alis

The breeze turns menacing,
treetops bend,
creak like our ship tossed on the waves
those months at sea.

Alis

That evening,
Mother serves a watery pottage
while I hold sweet Samuel to my shoulder,
kiss him when the cottage shudders
with the lashing wind and rain.
Father does not eat.

"What is it, Dyonis?" Mother says.
She takes his hand in hers.

"The Governor's assistants have talked.
We've asked him to leave with Ferdinando
once all our goods are onshore."

I cannot believe what Father is saying.
Governor White must go
With our mutinous pilot?
The man who's anchored here
for these five weeks,
who's been no help
removing our possessions?
Who's offered us no shelter
in the midst of our enemies?

The words spill from me.
"You want the Governor to desert us."

Samuel's face reddens.

He opens his mouth to howl.
Mother takes him from me,
gathers him in her arms.

"If he doesn't go to England,
how will Sir Ralegh learn
what's happened?" Father says.

No good has happened here,
but to have our leader go,
to believe he must—
My insides knot;
I can't imagine eating
this scant meal.
Outside the wind screams,
echoing the eerie songs
of the Roanoke.

"The Governor said no.
He's worried it will seem
he's abandoned us."
Father pounds his fist on the table.
The bread plate clatters.
"What does it matter how things appear?
Would he have us die
to keep his reputation?
Ferdinando wouldn't bother telling
we're at Roanoke
and not Chesapeake.
The Governor must be the one

to ensure the supply ships find us.
We'll have to bribe the pilot
to take Governor White at all."

"Dyonis," Mother says,
her voice high,
light like a melody,
"Remember Alis."

"Mother, I've seen everything you have!"

I think of Kimi.
I've seen more
than Mother knows.

"And what of that savage man?" Mother asks.
"Does he stay or go?"

"He stays as Lord of Roanoke Island,
as our connection to the Indians
and the Queen's representative."

Mother stands
abruptly,
snatches away
the bread plate.
"I do not trust him," she says.

Alis

All night,
our home is cuffed by violent winds
and waves of rain,
a hurricane.
This settlement will fly apart,
will be ripped like weeds,
until each board is stripped away.

This village is as fragile as an egg
unprotected in its nest.

I pray
for peace
and silence,
for just an hour of rest.

KIMI

The lashing winds
strip the bark from our longhouses.
The second-planting corn bends its head,
weeping for the harvest
that will never come.

But we are safe
here in our village.
This is enough.

Wanchese says the English
know nothing of the hurricane's might,
and his men pound their heels on the earth,
raise their gourd rattles,
sing for their destruction.

Alis

Like the becalmed winds,
I'm less anxious now.
We,
all of us,
pick through the ruins from yesterday's storm:
the reeds torn from rooftops,
doors thrown across the common,
benches piled like street rubbish,
branches strewn everywhere.

I gather wood
knowing Father and the other assistants
are talking to the Governor,
demanding he desert us so he might
    direct supply ships,
    ask for help moving to Chesapeake,
    beg for rescue from the quick foes we've made.

George waits at the barracks
where they're sequestered,
acts as messenger
to tell us news,
but as of yet,
there is none,
only a silent building.

Then Mr. Dare
opens the door

and signals to George,
who runs from woodpile to woodpile
spreading latest word.
His freckled cheeks
are burned a deepened red.
Before he reaches me,
I know what he will say.
The men have come to an agreement.

There is no turning back.

Alis

I remind Mother of the berries
the day we came,
and she allows me to search for them,
if I stay close to the boys who are hunting.
George assures her I'll be safe.
No Indians will approach us
with his musket near.

We pass Manteo,
who shores up the wall
now further damaged
from the wind and rain.
He nods to me,
and I to him,
a reminder of the secret we share.

Once we're beyond the gate,
I send the boys on,
for they are just as anxious
to be rid of me
as I am of them.
I pretend to search nearby
until they disappear.

KIMI

~~~

Footsteps fall
so close we might be seen.
I reach for Alis's hand,
pull her behind the huckleberry.

The English boys
swing their weapons side to side
as they lurch about.
No deer will approach
such movement and noise.

How serious they are,
trying on
the stern faces of men.
Hidden in the bushes,
I pretend I am one of them.
Alis bites her lips
to keep from laughing.

Alis

The boys pass by.
We climb high into a sprawling tree,
settle on a sturdy branch.
From here we can see everything.

The sunshine,
the dancing breeze,
I cannot help but swing my legs.

KIMI

Alis hums,
her music
strange and beautiful.
I use my voice to follow.

So rich her sounds
that echo mine.
I stop my song to listen.
Kimi's music fades.
"No," I say.
"Please sing again."

I lift my voice
in harvest songs,
a sad lament,
a child's simple melody.

My skin prickles as though from cold,
though sunlight pours down on me.

Never have I heard
such grace, such mystery.

> In this moment,
> all is right,
> all is just
> as it should be.

KIMI

The boys approach.
We scramble down,
rush to fill our bowls with berries.

"Good-bye," Alis whispers,
leaves our hiding place,
calls to the boys to wait.

Alis

Ferdinando and the Governor
will sail on the morrow.

I write to Joan,
try to describe
this remarkable world.
I do not speak of hardship,
only the sharp ocean air,
my baby Samuel,
the blue bird that makes a home here.
I cannot mention Kimi.

Fathers encourage sons
to send letters, too,
for their mothers to learn of their safety,
for a small measure of comfort.
Will they tell what happened
with Mr. Howe?
How our men mistakenly fought
our only friends?

And what of George?
Is his mother back in England,
hoping for news of their arrival?
I shudder to think of the message
he might compose,

then shake my head,
remember him marching with that musket,
anger dancing in his eyes.
Surely it is better
no one sends her word.

Alis

The Governor,
bedecked in his finest clothing,
proclaims to all
his intention to sail away,
tell of our difficulties,
send back supplies and more settlers
next spring, the earliest moment
ships can come again.

Though the assistants voted for this,
the faces of those around me
show not everyone is pleased
with his leaving.

Governor White acts
as if it's his idea to go,
he says,
come spring, the rest of us
will sail to Chesapeake,
leave Manteo behind
to rule for England.

"There is one thing
I must tell you," the Governor says.
He hesitates and starts again.
"I can't go without your knowing."

Like the winds that hinted at the hurricane,

whispers stir the crowd,
and all shove closer to the Governor,
whose wearied eyes
are those of an old man.

"My last time here,
we struggled with the Roanoke.
Our soldiers attacked their camp,
beheaded their leader, Wingina."

My heart beats
wildly within me.

"In haste we sailed home,
not knowing
a new ship had left
with more soldiers to be stationed here.
I prayed we would find them safe."
He says no more,
his shoulders hunched like one defeated.

Father strides to his side.
"Why did you
not speak of this
sooner?"

"At first, there was no reason.
We were bound for Chesapeake,
where new land, different tribes awaited,
a chance to start anew.

But when Ferdinando left us,
I did not want to frighten,
prayed for an opportunity to make peace."
His voice quakes.
"It was a foolish hope."

"No harm will come to us
while I am here," Manteo says.

Father laughs.
"What power do you have,
one man against two tribes?"

"I have gone to the Croatoan,
explained our mistake.
My people won't try again to harm us
as they did that day onshore."

"He's the Queen's man,"
the Governor says.
"Three years I've trusted him."

"And how does that
protect us?" Father says.

The Governor strokes Virginia's cheek,
who's cradled in his daughter's arms.
"If there is any reason
for you to leave
before my homecoming,

carve where you've gone
on the trunk of a tree.

If there's any sort of danger," he says,
quietly this time,
"include a cross in your carving."

He knows we are not safe here,
yet he departs,
abandons us
to Roanoke.

KIMI

All but the small boat
sail to deepest waters.
The men watch the village,
say the English remain.

It is a comfort knowing
my friend stays near.

Alis

It consumes me,
the attack the Governor
spoke of just this morning
before he sailed away.

Here,
in the quiet,
I must try
to make sense of things.

"Wingina?"

"Kimi, please tell me
what happened
before we came."

KIMI

Her face is grave
as she greets me.

It pierces me
to hear her say
my father's name.

I cannot make out
all her words,
but see the sorrow heavy
on her brow.
I use my hands
to paint pictures.

"Wingina. Alawa.
They are gone."
My palms
upturned
toward the sky.

Her hands are empty.
Her eyes fill with tears.

"The soldiers?" I whisper,
moving my fingers
like a consuming flame.

"Wanchese's fire?"
I show her of the burning,
those who escaped
to the canoes.

Her words and movements
confirm every awful thing.

Tears spill down her cheeks.
Did the attack take someone
dear to her?

The English,
my countrymen,
have brought upon the Roanoke
the same fear and horror
we feel for them.

These Englishmen
know nothing
of what happened?

"A Roanoke man."
I hold one arm straight ahead,
draw the other back.
"He had an arrow.
How it frightened me."

"Chogan."
I don't believe
he would have harmed her,
an unprotected girl,
but how can I know
if she was truly safe?
When friends
become enemies
how quickly
things can change.
Didn't the very man
who gave Alawa her ribbon
later attack my village
the day Wingina died?

It has been one life for another.
Death on both sides.

The English
have wronged us.
But there is suffering
we have also waged.

Alis

It's been three days
since the Governor left us,
and things are different now.

People group together,
scattered in bands across the common,
huddles that form and break,
reform again.
They stoke fears,
nurture worries,
imagined threats the center
of every conversation.

Community chores that once happened
without direction
have begun to dwindle,
each family looks
to protect its own members,
each man focuses only on himself.

Father speaks
of a Roanoke attack
to any who will listen.
Already,
he's drawn many to his side.

KIMI

"You wear your pearls so beautifully."
Mother pauses in her weaving.
"Such a strong woman you've become."

She straightens the strand about my neck.
"Why is it then you sometimes leave
the fields before the others?"

Mother thinks I've been idle,
but never have I worked so faithfully.
"I move quickly about my tasks
weeding and tending."

So I might go to Alis.

Mother doesn't answer
but her eyes never leave me.

Our women are woven together
in ways that form a dance.
It is difficult to step
outside
without breaking the pattern,
upsetting the rhythm.

I must not draw
Mother's further notice.

KIMI

Each day,
the English boys
march through the forest.
Their guns swing toward all sound,
as though danger lurks nearby.

It is the deer they're after.
I've seen enough
to know they sometimes make a kill,
but they also circle closer to our borders,
hint at an attack.

I have overheard my uncle
speaking with his men.
An opportunity will arise, he says,
the perfect time to show our might.

If these boys fear my people striking,
if they long to fight,
their wait is almost done.

Alis

The boys
roam each afternoon,
act as if they're hunting,
though it's Indians they want to find.

KIMI

What can I give Alis
that will show her she's my friend?
What might teach her
she's helped ease my pain?
What will guard her
from what Wanchese has planned?

I touch the pearls at my neck,
remember the pride I felt
when Mother gave them to me,
her tears warming my skin
as I left childhood behind.

What more than these?

There is nothing dearer to me,
save the memories of my sister.
For her I could do nothing.

The wooden bird
brought the two of us together,
but will it protect Alis?

This montoac,
what good is it,
if I leave her helpless?

September 1587

Alis

Mother shakes out an apron,
her golden hair swept back,
her blue eyes full of light.
She hums as her iron glides.
Her strength since Samuel's birth has returned.

"What is that noise?"
She peers out the window.
There is such commotion,
I open wide the door.

"Indians!"
George rushes through the village,
hollering so loudly,
Virginia startles in her cradle,
Samuel begins to cry.

"I was hunting,"
he says to those who've gathered.
"Ran back when I saw them."
George stumbles to a nearby bench,
sweat rolling down his face.
"Two other boys are out there still."

Long into the evening,
men swarm about with muskets,
trickle through the palisade,
searching for the others.

George is never far from Manteo,
as if the two patrol together.
But when George steps behind him,
though he does not fire,
he trains his musket
on the Indian's back.

Alis

Mr. Dare said
now that he's a father,
he couldn't rest until
those missing boys were found.

Mr. Dare was
with the first who checked
the woods outside our borders.

He has not
yet
returned.

Alis

I wake to shouts outside our window,
torches flickering past.
Father jumps from bed,
rushes outside.

"Mother?" I call.

"I'm here, darling."

I climb into the warmth
Father has left behind.
Mother strokes my hair,
Samuel nestled between us.
I pull close to her,
try to block the ever-rising voices.

Father bursts through the door.
"The boys are safe,
said they lost their way,
but Dare,"
Father stops,
cleans his throat,
"he's been
shot through
with arrows."

Alis

All are screaming,
rushing, running
to the square.

Two men drag his feet,
arrows buried in his chest.

"Ananias!"
Mrs. Dare falls to the ground
beside her husband's body,
her sleeves thicken with his blood.

It is daybreak
before Mother can persuade her
to hold her wailing child.

KIMI

All day is spent
in feast and celebration.

My people deserve peace.
But I no longer believe
war is the only way
to find it.

KIMI

Wanchese says
we teach our enemies their wrongdoings,
demonstrate the errors of their ways,

like the man he killed
after Wingina was beheaded,
and the fire he set
that frightened the others away.

Did the English understand?
For they came back again.

There was the man who hunted crabs.
How quickly he was slain.
Yet the English have remained.

Now our men celebrate
the man killed in the forest.

But this I wonder:
If the English
know nothing of our purpose,
these lessons are lost on them,
mean no more than
violence like their own.

Alis

I stroke my brother's cheek,
place my thumb in his palm.
His soft fingers wrap around mine,
his feet kick as he laughs.

Virginia is
without a father now.

Since his death,
even through his burial
near the bones and Mr. Howe,
Mrs. Dare has worn the dress
stained with her husband's blood.

Alis

Mother bustles into our cottage,
allows the door to slam behind her.
Both my hands fly to the cradles to keep the babies still.
Her face is hardened in a way I've never seen.

She bangs her bowl on the table,
kneads at dough so roughly
I am certain it is overworked,
will never start to rise.

My shoulders ache with rocking,
yet I dare not let the babies stir,
for I will not miss this chance to speak.

"What is it?" I whisper.

"Leave it be, Alis."
Her response stings;
my gentle mother doesn't speak like this.

"I'm no longer a child.
If it's about our village,
it does concern me."

Mother's eyes grow wide at my impudence,
narrow just as quickly.
"Very well," she says slowly,
"if you must know,

there's talk of Manteo amongst the women.
Mrs. Archard and I believe he's against us."

"What do you mean?"

Mother stops her kneading,
tucks a honeyed strand of hair beneath her kerchief,
pulls a chair from the table.
"You are too young to make sense of this."

"Mother," I say,
"you cannot keep the truth from me."
Few things go unnoticed here,
a reminder I must take care
with the secrets I keep.

Mother strokes Samuel's wispy hair.
"Your father says Manteo
was the last to return
the night Mr. Dare was slain.
Manteo said he was searching for the boys,
but they'd already found their way home."
She pinches her lips together,
her face as stern as Mrs. Archard's.
"It makes me wary.
Just how loyal can a savage be?"

But I know I trust him.
Manteo lets me go to Kimi,
has kept this to himself.

"For whatever reason,
he has cast his lot with us."

Mother shakes her head.
Her silence speaks more disapproval
than words ever would.

Alis

Toward evening the sun relents.
I carry Virginia to her home,
tap the door with my shoe.
Mrs. Dare opens,
her face blank and empty.
Dark stains still reach beyond her elbows,
stiffening the fabric of her threadbare sleeves.

So distant she seems.
If I give Mrs. Dare the baby,
will she remember to care for her?

"Perhaps I should keep her longer,
let you get your rest?"

She shakes her head,
reaches for Virginia.
Reluctantly,
I give the baby to her mother.

For a moment,
I linger in the doorway,
watch the sun
fade from the sky.
Someone grasps my hand,
turns me around.

"You've been outside the palisade," George says.
"After I've warned you."

My mind races.
Has he seen more?
Why did I ever
speak to him of Kimi?

"Perhaps your father should know."

"No," I say,
"there is no need."

He studies me closely.
I read a wisp of worry on his face.
"Be careful, Alis."

Alis

I become skilled at deceiving my parents:
snatching moments
once Father departs to work metal in his shed,
once Mother has left with laundry
for the unmarried men.

As for the babies,
young Miss Lawrence
agrees to do her mending
in Mother's rocking chair;
Mr. Florrie is happy to rest
on the bench outside our doorway,
prop his hairy arm upon our windowsill,
his hairier chin cupped in his hand.

I pretend I must fetch water,
remove laundry from the line.
Instead I leave the village,
quickly steal away.

Alis

She teaches me
which roots to eat,
how to weave a basket bowl,
where to find the sweetest berries,
that crabs keep a tidy home.

What marvelous things
Kimi has helped me see.

KIMI

Knowing her
enriches every ordinary moment,
makes each sorrow easier to bear.

Yet how long
can friendship
truly remain hidden?

Must we
someday
bring this
to an end?

Alis

Someone knocks
as I wipe the table.
Mrs. Dare is at our threshold.
She wears something clean at last.

"I support you," she says to Father.
"I'll do what is necessary."
She clasps his hand,
pulls the door behind her.

I glance at Mother,
try to read in her expression
what this means.
But she will not meet my eye.

Alis

It has been one week
since Governor White's leaving.
Most have assembled,
but there are some
who have chosen to be absent
for the meeting the assistants have called.

George and his band of boys
roam the square unattended.
Father calls the group to order,
and though voices fall,
the shouts of George's boys
continue unchecked.

"While we anticipate the Governor's return,
our future is uncertain," Father says.
"Our circumstance has worsened:
each day less food,
division amongst us,
unrest outside our borders."
His voice drops.
"The death of Ananias Dare."

Mrs. Dare's face is ashen.
Father moves to stand beside her.
"Governor White confessed
we live near Indians who've hated us
long before we anchored here."

Manteo speaks.
"I have gone to the Roanoke.
I've talked with them,
as I did my people."

"I do not trust this man!"

The woman's words are full of hate.

I turn to see who speaks.
It is Mother!

"Why would Manteo side with us?" she says.
"He could favor the Roanoke!"

The gathering's set ablaze.
"... this place is cursed ..."
       "... my son only talks of fighting Indians!"
"... hardly any flour left ..."
       "... Manteo, I cannot trust him ..."
"... don't know why we ever came."

"Enough!" Father roars.
One word reaps silence.
"We must prepare to leave for Chesapeake."

There are cries of gratitude.
Mother embraces Mrs. Dare,
the babies between.
I cannot help but edge away from their joy,
the ugly power of Mother speaking.

"The Governor thinks it best
to delay until spring," Manteo says.

Father's mouth is firm.
"John White is gone.
All he offered us
was false security.
Who will leave with me?"

Men and women ease toward Father.
Several draw close to Manteo.
A few stay where they are.

I am pulled in all directions:
finding safety,
losing Kimi.
This division in our midst.
Where do I belong?

Alis

Father insists
we desert
this prison,

this place
whose beauty
sings within me.

Alis

Manteo and I,
we have a pattern now.
I check to see no one is near,
walk slowly to his guard post.
He signals when the way is clear
of Englishmen or Roanoke
that I might go to Kimi.

Today,
her eyes are troubled.
Something smooth
like weathered pebbles
is cupped in her palm.

Kimi touches my forehead,
brings our hands to my heart.
Her pearls are sea foam
spilling from her fingers.

"Montoac," she says,
placing them over my head.

She gives this to me?
Montoac.
It is what she called
Uncle Samuel's bird.
What might it mean?
I try to piece ideas together:

Gift?
Token?
Treasure?
All feel right.

I run my finger around the strand.
"Thank you," I tell her,
touched by her generosity.
I reach for Uncle's bird,
something I might give her.
I hold it out.
She pushes it away.

"Montoac," she whispers,
her eyes unblinking.

I think she wants
to hear me say it.
"Montoac," I answer.

The word
brings her
relief.

KIMI

Alis tucks my rope of pearls
inside her coverings.
And though its beauty is hidden,
it is right for her to do.

Every day, the risks
we take are greater.
There, close to her heart,
my montoac will protect her
from what Wanchese
surely plans.

Alis

The sun has moved beyond the tallest trees.
It is later than I've intended.

Racing through the forest,
I hear footsteps behind me.
The Indian again?
The pearls thump against my skin,
warmed as if they are a part of me.

I squeeze between the palisade,
scramble over the earthen wall,
desperate to escape whoever is so near.

"Who's there?"
Old Lump-and-Bump lumbers into view.
"Miss Harvie?" he says,
"What do you think you're doing?"

"Catching a breath of air?"
The story is ridiculous even to my ears.

Lump-and-Bump towers above me,
his knobby nose on great display.
"Do not tell me
you've not been warned
of the dangers outside."

I drop my chin to my chest.

"Mr. Bailie!"

Old Lump-and-Bump looks about.
Outside the village,
two hands cling to the embankment,
a sunburned face appears.

George.
He was the one
out there.

He jumps over the wall.
"I saw Alis,"
he's out of breath,
"while I was hunting."

When did he notice me—
before or after I left Kimi?

"Let's see what your father thinks,"
Old Lump-and-Bump says.

Alis

He marches me to the ironmonger shed,
where Father's hammer bangs.
George follows behind.

Alis

Inside
there is darkness and fire,
Father's shape beside the flames.
"Roger, what is this?"
He wipes his hands
on a cloth tucked at his waist.

Only when he is near us
can I see his grim expression.

Old Lump-and-Bump shoves me forward.
"I caught your daughter scrambling over the wall."

Everyone
so close,
the air bears the odor
of sweat-soured clothing.

Father's eyes hold mine,
daring me to glance away.
My teeth clamp down.
I will say naught.

"Alis betrayed us," George says.

I lean against the wall,

Father frowns.
"What do you mean?"

 will my heart to calm.

"Ask her what she was doing
in the forest just now."

Alis

"Alis?"
All eyes are with me.
"What is this George says?"

"I do not know."

"Speak of the girl,"
George's lips are hardly moving,
"or I will do it for you."

"Girl? Alis is the only one
amongst us," Father says.

George lunges toward me.
There's hatred in his eyes.
"Tell your father!"

I press my fingers
to my face.
I thought George was my friend.

"A Roanoke girl," I say.

Alis

"An Indian?"
Father's expression says
I'm not his daughter,
but a stranger.

For an eternity
he looks from George to me.

"You've threatened our safety."

"Father, no!"

He whips me around,
forces me to keep in step
as he pulls me from the shed.

"I've brought us no harm!
She's just a girl,
like me."

Alis

George saw us together.
Did he hurt her after I'd gone?

Outside our doorway Father stops,
twists my arm until it pinches.

Anger's etched upon his ruddy face.
But it's the way Father's mouth turns down
that says fear's what truly plagues him.

"Alis?"
Miss Lawrence opens the door,
Samuel in her arms.
He wails,
waves his tiny fists.

"What story did she tell you?
Surely not the truth,
that she went to meet an Indian."

Pricks of crimson flood
Miss Lawrence's cheeks.
She fumbles for the door.

Father slams it shut behind her,
and now Virginia's crying.
"How dare you," he says,
each

word
ablaze.

"You said yourself how lonely
it must be as the only girl.
And Kimi—"

"Enough!"

I fight to catch my breath,
swallow the sob rising within me.
Kimi.
Father.
There's not one thing
I haven't damaged
today.

KIMI
~~~

I do not know what I will say
to explain my missing pearls.
Without them, I should feel naked,
like a child who still plays
at her mother's feet.

Before the sickness,
Alawa and I
had dreamed of the tattooing,
copper dancing at our earlobes,
the blessings given to those
leaving childhood.
What pride we imagined
in passing through the ceremony.

I never called out
in pain when the ink
marked me
as separate from the little ones,
pointed to my life ahead.

Yet never have I felt
more brave than now.
Alawa,
though you never lived to see,
you must understand:

Today
I left my younger self
behind.

I have given my pearls away,
sacrificed my montoac,
removed my own protection
to cover my friend.

KIMI

I make no effort to hide
how bare I am.
Mother rushes to me,
pulls at my hands,
only to find them empty.

I will not lie,
but I will not bring
Alis danger.

"Your pearls?"

"Gone," I say.
Though my voice quakes,
there is no shame,
no apology,
no sorrow.

What I've done
is best for Alis.

I glide past my aunts and mother,
am first to begin the evening meal.

KIMI
~~~

Their whispered words—
How careless, they say.
My aunts' open stares.

I will endure them,
do my work.
Even as the young ones
swarm about with questions,
I will not say a word.

Alis

Later,
Father grips my shoulders,
his hands blackened from labor.

"I've told the assistants
of your foolishness.
Soon everyone will learn
my daughter,
whose own uncle
faced a Roanoke attack,
the very one who cares for Ananias Dare's child,
placed us in danger
by befriending our enemy.

It won't surprise me in the least
if Mrs. Dare holds you responsible
for her husband's death."

My heart is
tender as a bruise.

"How could you do this?" he whispers.

Does he truly want an answer?
That she has eased my heartache,
shown me things I've never known,
these reasons aren't enough for him,
they wouldn't satisfy.

"Do not leave this house again.
Not to fetch Virginia,
not to wander in the village.
You stay inside."

I nod my head,
pinch my lips together.
I will let him see
the pain this causes me.

Alis

From the window,
a blue bird flits
from roof to bench to branch.

The pearls are heavy at my neck,
tucked beneath my clothing.
Father can keep me locked away,
but he can't force me to forget
the new world opened to me.

Alis

Ia-chá-wan-es,
Kimi's word echoes
the pulse in my fingers,
the bird's beating wings.

Ia-chá-wan-es,
I whisper to Samuel,
I hum its bright music,
its melody sings.

I hold the name closely,
its beauty my treasure,
hidden here with me,
my secret alone.

Alis

Mother,
always so quick
to mend any rift
within our family,

after Father whispers to her
all that's happened,
looks to me,
disappointment in her eyes.

She says
nothing,
does
nothing
to make things better.

Never
have I been
more alone.

KIMI

~~~

The day passes
with sun and dirt and weeding.
I leave the fields,
I go to find her,
but she is not in our meeting place.
I reach for my pearls,
remember they are gone.

Though I do not know
Wanchese's plans,
I will not believe
she is in danger,
for my montoac protects her.

I could do nothing for Alawa,
but I will do all I am able
to keep Alis safe.

Alis

Mrs. Dare no longer
brings Virginia.
She does not trust me
with her child.

As Father suggests,
am I to blame
for Mr. Dare's death?

It is
too much—

Did I destroy
this family?

Alis

Shut in,
I will not wander,
will not talk
to those I shouldn't.

Unseen,
I will not bring
my family
further shame.

Closed off,
held back,
contained,
I will not tempt
disaster.

Forgotten,
I will
simply
fade away.

Alis

Though a few still side with Manteo,
most assistants want to leave at once.
We are so close to Chesapeake,
they say,
the journey will be swift,
that shelters, a few vegetables
are a poor excuse for staying
where our very lives are threatened.

Father was the one
who pushed for leaving sooner,
but this has been forgotten.
He's been stripped of his position.
No one listens to him now.

His daughter is a traitor, they say.

Alis

At first,
we'll take
only what's necessary.
Later,
others will collect
the rest of our possessions.

What do I have that is needed,
save the clothing I wear?
Yet there is one here
far more dear to me than these.

We will depart,
sail in the pinnace,
group by group,
build the City of Ralegh.

We are to forget this Roanoke,
but I cannot,
I never will.

Alis

"We're to gather in the square
this evening," Father says.

I stir my pottage,
more water than true meal.
For once I am not saddened
Father keeps me shut away.
I could not bear
their questioning eyes,
their looks of disapproval.

"You're coming, Alis," he says.

I grip my spoon so tightly,
it bites into my skin.
"What do you mean?"

"You'll tell everyone you forsake that Indian."

I glance at Mother.
She never turns my way.

"If you don't," he says,
"we'll be outcast,
unable to start again in Chesapeake."

I slam the spoon upon the table,
hoping for correction.

Mother hasn't spoken to me in days.
Instead she stands,
swiftly clears the table.

Father pushes back his chair.
"It's time to go," he says.

Alis

How different the outside world is,
how unfamiliar the village seems,
the night air not as I remember it,
the stars in unknown patterns,
these faces strange.

So much feels changed
in just three days.

Father moves ahead of us.
I stay with Mother,
her body shields me from the others.
If only she'd speak,
put her arm about my shoulders.

The talk is as it's always been—
threat and leaving,
hunger, fear.

Then Father calls to everyone,
"My daughter wants to speak."

Everyone staring,
fire and shadow
in their faces.
I try to breathe.
My chest is pinched.

"Tell them, Alis."
Father's words ring out.

Kimi,
my friend,
who's been
so good to me.
I twist my apron
in my fists.

Now Father's next to me.
"Say it," he says.

"I—"
my throat constricts.
No words will come.

"You must," he whispers.

My family's standing
rests on this.

Forgive me, friend.
What else can I do?

"I was wrong."
The words come,
but I will not claim them.
"I betrayed our village
in befriending the girl."

No one speaks.

Mother's eyes are downcast.

No one
says a thing
because
they'll
never
trust me.

My heart rushes.
I crush my hand against it.
And feel them.
Kimi's pearls.

It is too much!
Tears prick my eyes.
I've given her away.

Alis

Those who call me traitor,
there is no reason
they'll embrace me
once we set sail for Chesapeake.

They will all begin again.
I will still be a disgrace,
a reminder
of strife
and fear
and failure.

Alis

I cannot sleep,
ask Father for a bit of wood.
I do not have Uncle's skill,
am not so familiar with iacháwanes
to remember every feature,
but what I create satisfies.

I imagine Uncle Samuel,
his warm hand at my back,
and the making
helps ease my grief
in losing him,
helps me forget for just a moment
I've lost her, too.

"It is good," Father tells me as he holds it.
"Fine work like Samuel's."

He talks as though
all is well between us.

This bird's a humble offering,
though she'll never receive it.
This bird speaks the things I cannot say.
I am sorry, Kimi.
I knew no other way.

KIMI

Though she hasn't come,
each day I go to meet her.

Is she safe?
Does my montoac
protect her?

Or has she decided
our friendship is a burden,
the risk of knowing me
too great?

Alis

Father says
my confession
has set me free,
that with time
I'll be forgiven
by the community.

Mother speaks
to me again,
but uses formal words,
that help to keep her distance.
She has no soft caresses,
no tenderness for me.

Perhaps one day,
Father will again be asked to lead.
Perhaps Mother will soften,
that all she needs is time.

Neither understands
why I remain indoors.

I cannot undo
what I've done
to Kimi.

I cannot face
those who do not
want me near.

Until we leave the island,
this is where I'll stay.

Alis

This truth is inescapable:
living here brings danger.

      I imagine meeting Kimi
      in a place we mustn't hide.

It never was expected
we'd remain on Roanoke.

      If we had never journeyed here,
      how much my life would lack.

We are impoverished,
desperate.

      I'm most myself
      when with her.

How might I find peace
when two worlds war inside?

Alis

How many days
since George saw
the two of us together?
Perhaps a week or more.
It is hard to remember,
too painful to think upon.

Even inside the cottage
The heat has relented a mite,
the morning air does not press down
like such a heavy weight.
Summer's end draws near.

Outside,
The men drag trunks,
roll barrels through the village
to the pinnace at the shore.

It happens so suddenly,
the shouts that pound like thunder,
pulling all to the square.

From the window
I see Father,
unsteady on his feet,

lunging
at
Manteo.

Alis

I forget my vow to stay inside,
race to see what happens.

Alis

Mr. Pratt
and Old Lump-and-Bump
try to restrain Father,
but they're no match for his fury.

"Speak!" he yells to Manteo,
"of the attack you've planned
with the Roanoke!"

Alis

"I can tell you."
George smiles.
Never have I seen him more satisfied.
"Manteo meets in the forest
with them."

Father's neck is mottled red.
"There is no reason for this boy to lie!"

"I've planned no attack," Manteo says.
But others badger from the crowd,
call for Manteo's arrest.

"You refuse to help us load the pinnace,
insist we stay though Howe and Dare are dead.
You want to fight with the Roanoke against us,
rid Virginia of all Englishmen."

"Am I not an Englishman?" Manteo says.

"Your hair.
These beads about your neck."
Father yanks the strand.
Shells spill to the ground.
"No Englishman dresses this way."

Manteo's teeth are clenched
though his words are clear.

"Do you not realize
how much I've lost in joining you?
Some here do not trust me.
My own people
do not understand.

But they have not seen what I have,
our queen,
Elizabeth,
the great weroansqua,
whose power reaches across the seas.

I can be Croatoan,
and speak for my people.
I can be an Englishman,
and serve my queen."

"Liar!"
Mrs. Dare shouts,
"Spy!"

It is George who yells the loudest,
his features a grotesque mask of hate.

The tumult grows,
explodes into a frenzied chorus.

Alis

I set my feet wide
to keep from being shoved about.
Mother finds me,
Samuel's cries reaching hysteria.
She pleads with me to follow,
but I pretend I can't hear her.

Mr. Pratt and Lump-and-Bump
have tied Manteo's hands behind him.
His head dips forward
like a broken reed.

I try to piece together
what George might have seen,
if what he said is true.
George would gain satisfaction
in finding reason to attack.

At Father's command,
the men lead Manteo to the jail.
How quickly Father's found his place again.

"Alis!" Mother calls,
but still I will not go to her
nor Father,
who has sparked unrest,
encouraged an angry boy
to speak against Manteo,

the one our Governor
appointed as our leader,
the one our Governor
called friend.

Alis

I return to our cottage,
close all the shutters
to escape the chaos outside.

"I called for you," Mother says.

I do not answer.

"Father's looking for the Howe boy.
Have you seen him?"

George is not my worry.
I care for nothing that happens
in this village anymore.

Mother finds a piece of bread,
serves me a modest portion.
My hunger awakens.
I've had nothing since breakfast.

I do not ask of Father,
simply reach for Samuel,
let his steady breathing
draw me to sleep.

Alis

It is Mother who awakens me
in the mid-afternoon.

"Please take this to your father.
He's had no food since morning."

Within me,
anger's fire has diminished,
leaving sorrow's blackened ash.

I hold the bread she offers,
kiss the top of Samuel's head.

KIMI

The sun escapes the clouds
that have held it fast.

There is change in the English camp,
the way they move about
like the sparrows that flock
just to flee
the harvest season.

The sun journeys farther
across the great expanse.

The English boy
whose hair curls at his forehead,
like strips of peeled river birch bark,
from behind a tree
I see him approach,
put down his weapon.

In watching Alis
I've come to understand
the English coverings
are for more than warmth and protection.
Maybe the boy has never seen
a woman dressed as I am.
I cross my arms before me
for his comfort.

"I've come to speak of Alis."

Hope soars
when I hear her name.

"We know of your secret meetings."
He hesitates for a moment.
"Don't expect her again."

What has happened
that she hasn't come?

"She is in trouble."
His eyes meet mine.
In a flash he lowers his gaze.
"I have caused her trouble."

I hold my fist to my chest.
"Alis."
Before this English boy
I claim her.

"There is something else," he whispers,
his features sharp with pain.
"I am sorry."
He covers his face.
"I am sorry!"

He rushes away.

Alis

There is one whose needs
might have been forgotten
in the chaos of the day.

I cross the threshold,
hold the bread in my outstretched hand.
"For Manteo."
My voice echoes off the walls.

Mr. Pratt wipes his bald head with a rag,
follows me with wary eyes.

"My mother sent me with this," I say,
for what is one more lie?
Mr. Pratt takes the bread,
pushes it through the iron bars.

Manteo lifts his head.
"Thank you, Alis."

This man
saw no wrong
in my befriending Kimi,
this one
who lives
in the in-between—
not of one world
or the other.

"You and your friend.
I made sure you
were always safe."

"Thank you," I whisper,
trust he feels the gratitude
these simple words convey.

Mr. Pratt crosses his arms.
"You've done what you came to do."
It's clear he wants me gone.
But there's one thing I must know.

I lean in close,
rest my forehead on cool metal.
"Why did you let me go to her?"

His long black hair,
pearls in his ears,
all is familiar now.
Manteo smiles faintly.
"Never would I alter
what is right."

KIMI

~~~

The boy looked
for me.

      I linger until all have eaten.
      The fire pops,
      sends up sparks
      that are swallowed
      before they reach the sky.

The boy came
to speak of Alis.

      "Uncle."
      The name binds us.
      He cannot turn
      his brother's child away.

      "Kimi," Mother scolds.
      "Leave our weroance alone."
      I will not listen.

The boy took
great risk in coming.

"Uncle."
I lift my chin,
launch the word like an arrow.
"Go."

He cannot
refuse me
now.

KIMI

<u>~~~</u>

Wanchese's jaw tightens as he studies me.
I reach for my pearls,
now gone.

"They were our friends once," I say.

"The English?
Why do you
speak of them again?"

His words warn
not to push further,
but I do not heed them.

"I want to know
why things changed."

"You come to me
as though you have permission.
You forget I am weroance."

"You are Uncle."
This has never changed.

Wanchese sighs,
he thinks I haven't learned my place.
But I know exactly where I belong.
Here. Near him.
and with my dear friend, Alis.

"They only give false friendship,"
Wanchese says.
"If Wingina had listened
he would still be with us.
It was too late
when he saw as I did.
The path to his death
had already begun."

He leans closer.
His necklace flashes
in the firelight.
"Never forget
the English
killed your father."

I cannot help but say it.
"Not all of them
must be our enemies."

He gazes at the fire, silent.
It is only when I'm sure he's finished
that he speaks again.

"Have you gone to the English?"

"Uncle?"

"Have you spoken with them?"

How I want to tell of Alis,
that she's the friend I need.
That even if she's abandoned me,
I will never leave her.
But this truth is forbidden.

"Wanchese."
Nuna's father calls him.
"Chogan is missing."

My uncle stands to go,
but first turns back to me.
"Have you betrayed my trust?"

I cannot answer.
Behind us, I hear whispers.
It is Mother, her sisters.

Wanchese's eyes are cold, unfeeling.
"Do not be reckless.
This is not a game."

Alis

Our friendship,
it is right,
Manteo said.
I'll hold to this smallest comfort.
Someone understands.

The sun nears the horizon.
The village feels abandoned.
No one is about.
But there is someone
coming from beyond the forge.
George, lunging as if he's new to land
after months at sea.

"Where have you been?" I ask him.
Does he even hear me?

His musket trails behind him,
cuts a wavering line.

"I went to her.
I saw the girl.
Told her I am sorry."

He stumbles to the ground.
"Near their village.
I wanted to get close enough
to frighten them."

He makes an awful sound,
as though he is in pain.

"I've killed an Indian," he says.

KIMI

I leave the fire's circle,
its ring of light emboldened
now that dusk approaches.

"Kimi," Mother calls.
"It's time to eat."
She holds a bowl of fish in her hand.
But my thoughts are elsewhere.
The boy tried to tell me something,
and now Chogan is missing.

Already the men search the forest,
where Chogan hunted.
I remember the English boys
circling ever closer to our village,
their weapons always ready,
how sometimes we'd see them
from the shelter of the corn.

I run to the fields
before I know
exactly what I'm doing.

KIMI
~~

The third-planting corn's bright tassels
dance in the sun's last golden rays.
The air tinged with coolness
speaks of harvest coming soon.

Before I enter the fields,
my feet stop moving
over the packed earth.
Everything about me
stills.

There a man lies,
his arm twisted under him,
a gaping wound on his back.
Chogan.

Alis

"What did you say?"
Dread wraps about me.

His clothes are filthy.
His eyes are far away.
"I've killed an Indian."

"The girl?"
I cannot help
the anger in my voice.

He shakes his head.
"A man," he whispers,
leans his head on his knees.
"I want my father."
Sobs shake his body.
"I want him back again."

"What's this?" Mrs. Archard says,
walking past with young Tommy.
"Someone help this boy!"

Soon we are surrounded.

KIMI

I run the well-worn path
past the longhouses
to Wanchese,

fight for my breath,
tears blur my sight.

"Uncle!"

Wanchese hurries to my side.

"Chogan is dead."

KIMI

All rush
to the fields.
I wipe my face,
wait until they've gone.

And run.

KIMI

Wanchese
will keep
striking,

My legs burn,

he will
not stop,

my chest screams,

until the English
are destroyed.

Only once outside their palisade
do I allow myself to rest.

Alis

Mr. Archard and Mr. Florrie
lift George to a bench.
Mrs. Archard holds a cup,
insists he drink.

Father shoves past the others,
his shirttails flying,
rushes to the middle of the crowd,
his forehead lined
with soot and sweat.

"What has happened?" he demands.

I step back from everyone.
I do not want to know
what George might say.

I am finished
with the fighting,
the mistrust in the village.
Yet how will it be different
when we leave for Chesapeake?
With other tribes
it only seems
division will remain.

Our surroundings will be new,
but our fears will be the same.

KIMI

I have trusted my montoac
to protect her,
but to keep her truly safe,
I must tell the English
to leave immediately,

I must send her
away.

KIMI

The ditch,
the middle boundary,
provides cover in the coming darkness,
but I will not stay huddled there.

I dart from one building
to the next,
pushing closer
to the center
of the village,
crouch low
behind a house,
remove her ribbon
from my skirts,
knot it
about my wrist.

With this
I'll show her people
I come peacefully,
hope they'll listen
when I tell them
it's best for them to go
now,
quickly,
before it is too late.

KIMI

~~~

All the people crowd about,
surround a crying boy,
the one from the forest.
Desperate,
I search for Alis.

KIMI

Rough fingers
grasp
my wrist!

jerk
my arm,

spin me
around.

Alis

"I've caught an Indian
here in our village!"

The dusk's alive with voices
  ". . . others must be coming!"
  ". . . go find shelter!"
people scatter from the square.

Old Lump-and-Bump
leads Kimi
by the arm.

KIMI

The man pulls.
My feet do not behave.
So many of them fleeing,
open fear upon their faces.
My knees
cannot support me,

then I see Alis.

Alis

Kimi!
She's come to me.
Please, God, keep her safe!

I hold her gaze,
will her
not to worry,
though I know
in being here
I risk
everything.

I am
Wingina's daughter,
I am
Roanoke.
These things
give me courage.

Her shoulders back,
my ribbon wound
about her wrist,
she is so brave.

Father stands with George,
his hand on George's shoulder.
"Come, Alis," he says,
his eyes burning, insisting,
"this girl is nothing to you."

I will not live his lie again.
This time
I won't betray her.
From underneath my dress,
I pull her strand of pearls
from hiding,
walk a thousand steps
to reach her side.

How could I ever think
she had finished with me?

I touch my hand
to my head.
Touch it to my chest.

She reaches for me.
Our fingers intertwine.

I hold a fist
to my breast.
"Alis."
Sister of my heart.

Alis

We balance
on that edge
of time
before
all
collapses.

"Go," Kimi whispers to me.

"Go," she shouts.

Her voice rings out
for all to hear.

KIMI

The word's power
fills the air around us.
The English aren't the only ones
who can use their montoac.

Wanchese is coming,
I am certain of this.

The only way
to keep her safe
is to make her go.

Alis

Go.

The word's
permission.

It is
invitation,

freedom.
It's protection
from the danger
Kimi faces here.

I grip
her hand.

I didn't know
until this moment
this word
was what
I waited for.

Together,
we flee.

Alis

Tumbling,
the ditch catches us,
then running,
we pass through the palisade.

We fly
like blue birds
to the forest's embrace.

Alis

We duck
under branches,
weave
between trees,
travel
farther from those
calling
my
name.

I race
from their voices,
venture deeper
into the forest's shelter,
until
I can go
no
more.

KIMI

My word was meant
to keep her safe,
to send her elsewhere.

But she
chose
to go
with
me.

Alis

We rest for a moment,
under the low-reaching branches of a tree.
From my pocket,
I take the blue bird I've carved for her.
It's flawed,
this crude attempt,
the work of a beginner,
yet Kimi lifts it in the early moonlight,
holds it to her cheek.
"Iacháwanes," she whispers.

"Montoac."
My voice breaks.

KIMI

~~~

There are so many words
I do not have for her:

>   Nothing
>   to speak of comfort
>   to speak of courage
>   to speak of hope.

What I have is so little
but I give it still:

>   "Alis," I say.
>   Her eyes seek mine.
>   "Come home."

These are words she does not know.
Still she follows.

KIMI

We push forward
through the fast approaching darkness,
enter a clearing where
the moon hangs overhead.

And
then
they
come.

Hastily painted,
they storm
from the forest.

Bows,
quivers,
arrows,
they rush
to the English.

Alis cowers at my side.

Alis

We are surrounded!
Men painted in fearful patterns,
more threatening in these shadows,
arrows at the ready!

Is this how it
will end for me?

KIMI
~~~

From the ring of men around us,
this time Wanchese
calls to me.

"Kimi?"

"Yes, Uncle."
I tell my heart to steady.
Fear cannot rule me now.
"I have someone with me."

I step aside
so that all might see
Alis.

"An English girl?" he says.

"Alis. My friend."

She hears her name,
turns to me,
such trust in her eyes.
I will do everything
to keep her safe.

What strength it takes,
just being here.
Have I led her
just to bring her harm?

Wanchese
hates the English.

"Your friend."
His face hardens.

Alis

The man who speaks with Kimi
approaches me,
his face,
his arms,
his chest
awash with color.

He wears skins about his waist,
a chain of shells and copper beads.
I cannot help
how my body shakes.

He lifts his hand.
I duck,
expecting him to strike.

It is the rope of pearls he touches,
speaking to Kimi with words
I don't yet understand.

KIMI

"You gave this to her,"
Wanchese says.

"Yes, Uncle."

"You offered her protection."

He knows it to be true.

"What made you do this?"

What do I tell him?
Above,
two birds slip from a hollowed tree,
dance across the heavens.
Never have I seen iacháwanes
as the dark begins its path across the sky.
They've come to help me
make things plain.

Alis lifts her eyes to them.
A smile lights her face.

"Iacháwanes," I say.

The word is not an answer,
but something changes in him
as he watches us together,

something
tells me he sees:

Alis
belongs
with me.

Alis

Iacháwanes.
How gracefully they wing above,
how joyfully they scold,
they flit,
they chase.

The man studies the birds.
His sounds
bend, change shape
to words I understand.

"Many times Manteo has come,
asked for patience with your people.
He's promised they would leave
in the spring."

I stare.
This man speaks English?

"Is this when the English will go?"

Manteo speaking with this man,
is this what George saw?

KIMI

~~~

Manteo.
The Croatoan
so like the English.
Why does Uncle speak his name?

Alis

"They leave much sooner," I tell him.
"Days from now."
I focus on his eyes,
not on his fearsome paint.
"Most to Chesapeake.
Perhaps later,
some will go
to Croatoan with Manteo."

If he is released,
if they let him leave the prison.

KIMI

"This girl," Uncle says.

"Alis," I answer.

"Alis."

She hears her name,
reaches for my hand.
I squeeze it.

So often I longed
to tell Wanchese of her.
Now the moment has come.
"She is dear to me.
Please let her stay."

"You miss Alawa."

"I miss her every day."

"This girl,"
he pauses,
"Alis,
she's the one
who told you go."

"Yes."

Alis

The man turns to me again.
"Why should I trust
what you say about the English?"

"Because I've left them."
Though my voice wavers,
I must finish what I have to say.
"But I cannot leave Kimi."
These words finally make it true.

He looks to Kimi,
to me,
he speaks
to all the men.

They retreat.

Alis

These men
raced to destroy my village,

but Kimi
stopped them,

my words
turned them away.

KIMI

~~~

"Take Alis to your mother,"
Wanchese says.

Alis

Kimi insists on washing my feet,
leads me through the palisade
into her village.

The women sit about a fire,
follow us with their eyes.

Alis   # KIMI

A woman
holds her arms out,
pulls Kimi to her breast.

                    "Mother."

I see how
she strokes Kimi's cheek,
as my mother
so oft touched mine.

                    "I didn't know where
                    you'd gone," Mother says.
                    "And with Chogan dead . . ."

                    I lift my eyes to hers.
                    "I didn't mean to frighten you."

                    I'm so grateful
                    I can offer comfort.
                    "I have brought you someone.
                    Your daughter," I say.

                    "My daughter?"
                    Mother turns to Alis,
                    stares at this girl
                    with faded hair,

with water eyes.
I want Mother to see as I do.

"You were weaving.
You told me I was strong.
Do you remember this?"

"Yes," Mother says.

"I did not lose my pearls.
I gave them away."

"Why would you do
this?" Mother says.

"I chose to keep her safe.
Alis has left the English.
She has no one now."

Mother looks again to Alis,
pulls me close once more.
"My daughter," Mother whispers,
"you have made me proud."

Now,
with Kimi,
I am also in the woman's arms.
Great sobs rise up within me.
I have forsaken
Mother, Father, Samuel.

But I've protected them this way.

She kisses my hair,
tucks me under her chin,
makes the gentle noises
all mothers use
to soothe
a child's pain.

                        Their tears run together.

I cling to her,
this woman,
as I would my mother.
I weep
for all I've lost,
all I've given away.

Alis

They gather at the beach,
so ready for another place.
Have only two days passed?
Time is equal to forever
since I was last with them.

Father stands near the tree line
with Mother and Samuel.
One last time he calls to me,
though his face says
he expects no answer.
Mother wipes her eyes
on Samuel's swaddling bands.

Father pulls a knife from his waist,
uses it to mark the sand.
Mother lines the pattern with shells,
sobs as Father leads her
to the pinnace.

It is final,
my staying here.

The weight of my leaving
and all I have rejected,
this uncertainty
I will claim.

Kimi and I run to where they were,
examine what they together made.

A bird,
like Uncle's parting gift.
It is farewell and sorrow,
a final blessing,
hope and heartache.

A new beginning.

I belong
on Roanoke,
where Uncle lived
his final days.
The place
that brought me Kimi.

She clasps my hand.
I use the fist we've formed
to wipe my cheeks,
whisper my thanks
to her,
this girl who calls me sister.

Alis

I learn the rhythm
of the morning fields,
sunshine ripening
burnished corn,

the stillness
of the afternoons,
the coolness
of the shimmering stream,

the melody
of the evening—
mealtime voices,
the thundering fire,
the silent song of moon and stars
spread across the heavens.

How is this way of living new to me?
Its music
I have somehow
always known.

August 1590

Alis

It has been three summers
since English boats
have huddled near the beach
as they do now.

All night,
the men aboard
call to the shore,
their voices rise together.

>	Summer is a-coming in
>	Loudly sing cuckoo

The song,
it puzzles me.

>	Groweth seed and bloweth mead
>	and springs the wood anew
>	Sing cuckoo!

A memory
from another time.

"We are here!" their noises say.
"We're searching for our countrymen."

My mother worries
when I tell her I want to see them,
but Kimi understands.

———————

At dawn they come ashore.
I crouch behind reeds.
Their dark backs bob like driftwood
as they trudge from the beach.

How hot they must be
with such heavy clothing,
how odd to see again
whiskers on men's faces,
not smooth cheeks plucked clean.

Though curiosity sparks within me,
there's no desire to call to them,
show them I am near.
For this I fully understand:
The English are no longer mine.

The Governor is frailer now.
"Someone's been here.
These recent tracks
were left by Indians."

I see the marks he speaks of—
no impressions made with English shoes,
just footprints in the sand.

My own.

I follow the men to the village,
knowing rubble is all they'll find.
Those who went to Chesapeake
broke down houses,
barracks, forge
to use again.
Those few who went with Manteo
took all else left behind.

"They've disappeared," the Governor says,
"lost like the fifteen men."

Lost.
The word sounds strange,
for it doesn't speak of me.

Once,
I was a part of these people.
Three years have passed.
It was not long ago.

At times I ache
for Samuel,
Mother,

Father,
even George,
yet it is hard to remember
before Kimi was my sister,
Roanoke my world.

The men search the village.

"Croatoan!"
The Governor traces the letters
he finds on the palisade,
hope alight in his voice.
"Let us go to them."

I watch them
until I can no longer see,

inspect my naked feet,
brush the dirt from my soles,
in haste run to my village,
hurry to the place
I belong.

Glossary

Algonquian is a language family with over two dozen dialects. The following words from a now-extinct dialect would have been used by the Croatoan and Roanoke peoples.

iacháwanes—Eastern bluebird. John White's watercolor of iacháwanes is now at the British Museum and can be seen online:

> http://www.britishmuseum.org/research/collection_online/
> collection_object_detailsaspx?objectId=728253&partId=1&
> people=103070&peoA=103070-2-23&page=1

maquowoc—opossum

montoac—great spiritual power; mysterious power. An object could contain montoac and would benefit and strengthen its owner

weroance—chief or leader; literally means "he is rich," "he is of influence," or "he is wise"

weroansqua—female leader

Author's Note

Why do I write historical fiction? For the same reason I used to teach history. I'm nosey, plain and simple. While this is not an especially polite thing to admit about myself, it's what makes historical fiction a beautiful fit for me. Research lets me dig into other people's experiences and live in their world. It's a perfectly respectable way to satisfy my curiosity.

While teaching fifth-grade social studies in 2008, I rediscovered the mystery of England's first settlement—the unsuccessful one, what we now call the Lost Colony of Roanoke. Though our textbook devoted just a few small paragraphs to the Lost Colony, it was enough to stir my nosey side. When a student gave me a book called *National Geographic Mysteries of History*, which devoted a chapter to these English settlers, it was enough to seal the deal. I knew I'd write a book about Roanoke someday.

These are the things we know to be true:

In 1584, English explorers landed at Roanoke Island. Sir Walter Ralegh[1], a member of Queen Elizabeth's court, sponsored the voyage. A painter named John White was part of this first expedition, and he recorded much of what we now know of the plants, animals, and native people of that time. The crew returned to England with Manteo, of the Croatoan tribe, and Wanchese, a Roanoke, as ambassadors, as well as news of all they'd seen.

---

1 Elizabethan names were often spelled a variety of ways. Sir Walter used "Ralegh" most often in reference to himself.

In 1585, the English returned to Roanoke to build the fort we now call Fort Raleigh. They named the island and the surrounding land Virginia, in honor of the Queen. On the voyage were John White, Manteo, and Wanchese. Wanchese quickly returned to the Roanoke, but Manteo stayed on as interpreter. The English leaned heavily on their Roanoke and Croatoan friends, asking for food and assistance. Both tribes were supportive of the English at first, but backed away as their demands for food increased and illness spread to their people.

By the summer of 1586, when English privateer Sir Francis Drake stopped at Roanoke to check on the colonists, they jumped at the chance to leave with him.

Just six weeks later, the third group of English settlers arrived. They'd left England months before, planning to bring more soldiers and supplies to those at Fort Raleigh. They were amazed to find the fort abandoned, but left fifteen men to keep the fort in English hands.

Back in England, John White spent much of 1586 and early 1587 recruiting people interested in settling Virginia. During the 1585 journey, White and others had explored the mainland north of Roanoke, where they found fertile land and friendly people. The plan was to start fresh in this area with families this time. Still backed by Sir Walter Ralegh, this community would be named for him.

On July 22, 1587, 117 men, women, and children arrived in Virginia, ready to start the city of Ralegh in the Chesapeake Bay. But they were abandoned by pilot Simon Ferdinando on the island of Roanoke instead. These are the people we now know as the Lost Colony.

Upon their arrival, Governor John White found sun-bleached bones and the English fort empty. Vines grew through windows, and deer roamed the empty village. The colonists worked to make the fort livable for the coming winter and planned to relocate to Chesapeake in the spring.

On July 29, while crabbing, George Howe Sr. was killed by the Roanoke.

On July 30, John White, Manteo, and several of White's assistants sailed to Croatoan, Manteo's home. The English wanted to "renew the old love between us and them. . . and to live with them as brethren."[2] They asked the Croatoan to contact the Roanoke, telling them the same. How John White thought this might be possible is puzzling, for in 1586, after tension had built for months between the English and Roanoke, the English had attacked, beheading their weroance, Wingina.

From the Croatoan the English learned the Roanoke, led by Wanchese, had killed two of the fifteen English soldiers left on the island in 1586, trapped the others in a building, and set it on fire. The soldiers escaped and were last seen traveling north in Roanoke canoes.

The days passed with no response. Governor John White realized there was no friendship left to be recovered. He chose to attack. Twenty-seven men sneaked to the Roanoke camp in the early morning of August 9. But the Roanoke had fled. The Croatoan, who some historians believe had come early for the peace talks, were there instead, gathering

---

2 Lee Miller, *Roanoke: Solving the Mystery of the Lost Colony* (New York: Penguin, 2002).

the corn the Roanoke had left behind. Unknowingly, the English attacked their allies. Before it was all over, several Croatoan were dead.

Four days later, on August 13, Manteo was baptized as Lord of Roanoke and Desemunkepeuc, making a Croatoan the English ruler of these lands.

John White's granddaughter Virginia Dare was born August 18. Several days later, the Harvie family welcomed their own child.

By August 22, the colonists knew their situation was dire. They lived with hostile neighbors and had attacked their only allies. The supply ships that were to come the following year wouldn't know where to find them. The Governor's assistants begged John White to sail back to England with Ferdinando. He refused at first, probably because he feared it would look as if he'd deserted them. But the assistants insisted. Before the Governor's departure on August 27, he told the colonists if they left the island, they were to leave word of where to find them by carving their location on a tree. If they were in danger, they were to include a cross in their carving.

For three years, White tried to return to Virginia, but a war between England and Spain and several failed voyages kept him away. When he finally arrived off Roanoke's coast in 1590, sailors blew a horn and sang English songs far into the night. The following morning, White found the English village deserted. The buildings were gone. CRO was carved on a tree close to the beach. CROATOAN was left on a palisade pole. No cross was included with either engraving. The only recent sign of life was a footprint. White and his men returned to their ships, determined to sail to Croatoan. But a hurricane forced them out to sea.

Who were the people of the Lost Colony? They came from all walks of life—carpenters, smiths, and craftsmen—and were mainly middle-class residents of London eager to get away from the overpopulated, disease-laden, crime-ridden city. They knew nothing of Roanoke's history—and why should they? They were going somewhere else entirely.

In studying the names of passengers from the 1587 voyage, I noticed that of the eleven children listed, there were no girls. Why would that be? Were the girls left behind with their mothers to arrive at a later date? If a girl had come to Roanoke, what would it have been like to be the only one? I knew I wanted to explore a solitary girl character. Adding her to the Harvie family felt practical, as they'd have a built-in nursemaid.

Little has been recorded about the Roanokes' daily lives, though it is known women adorned themselves with tattoos (men wore tattoos on their shoulders to show which weroance they claimed). Both men and women wore jewelry. It is not too much of a stretch to assume the tattooing was part of a coming-of-age ceremony. I've taken the liberty of keeping the Roanoke in their island village in 1587 (where some lived in a satellite community during the summer months, but had abandoned sometime before Wingina's death, in an attempt to distance themselves from the English). Wingina and Wanchese were not related, though both served as Roanoke weroance. Kimi (meaning "secret") and Alawa ("little pea") are also my creation.

Why did Simon Ferdinando leave the colonists at Roanoke? No one really knows. Some historians think he wanted to raid Spanish ships before returning to England. Though White's records show he and Ferdinando argued throughout the voyage, why they argued is unknown. Historians generally agree John White was not the strongest of leaders. Perhaps the fate of the Lost Colony would have been different if White had stood up to Ferdinando.

What really happened to the Lost Colony? Though John White never saw them again, we know that at least some of them left Roanoke for Croatoan, if we take them at their word. Beyond that it's a mystery. There are plenty of theories: They sailed north to the Chesapeake and lived peacefully with tribes there, only to be wiped out by Chief Powhatan just before the founding of Jamestown, Virginia, in 1607; they were captured by mainland tribes and forced to work in copper mines; they intermarried with Manteo's people.

The last theory is supported by a remarkable piece of history: In 1703, a man named John Lawson was hired to survey North Carolina, the northern portion of the Carolina province, which was formed in 1629 and by this time included the islands Roanoke and Croatoan. He went to Croatoan (now Hatteras Island) and spoke with the people there. They told Lawson they had ancestors who dressed as he did and could also "talk in a book" (write).[3] And

3 John Lawson and William Byrd, *History of North Carolina* (Charlotte: Observer Printing House, 1903).

he noticed something that still intrigues me: A number of the Hatteras people had gray eyes instead of brown.

Were these people the descendants of the 1587 colonists and the Croatoan? What other explanation can there be?

Acknowledgments

I am indebted to all who have had a hand in the making of this book:

Michelle Humphrey showed me Kimi and Alis's friendship is the heart of this story. Thank you, Michelle, for helping me strip away what was unimportant and put my focus where it needed to be.

With her perfect combination of enthusiasm, knowledge, and support, Tracey Adams is exactly what I need in an agent. Here's to many years and many books together.

Stacey Barney's love for these girls was evident from the beginning and grew with each round of edits. Early on I asked her to push me hard to make this book shine, and she did just that. Stacey, I am so grateful for the privilege of working with you—an eight-years-in-the-making dream come true.

Kate Meltzer, Anne Heausler, Richard Amari, and the rest of the Penguin team contributed the behind-the-scenes touches that made this book just right. A special thank-you goes out to the folks in the school and library departments for their commitment to books like mine.

Anna and Elena Balbusso, I can't imagine a more beautiful cover. Thank you for bringing these girls to life through your artwork.

Reggie Brewer, Coordinator of Tribal Youth Programs and Cultural Enrichment for the Lumbee Tribe, and Steve Watts, Director of Aboriginal Studies at the Schiele Museum of Natural History in Gastonia, North Carolina, graciously read the manuscript for historical and cultural accuracy. Any errors that remain are mine alone.

Many thanks to Cultural Resources/Museum Manager Jamie Lanier, Geographic Information Systems Specialist Laura Pickens, and Park Ranger Rob Bolling at Fort Raleigh National Historic Site for answering my questions about the locations of the Roanoke and English villages.

Early feedback from friends and fellow writers Anna Ingwersen, Cynthia Leitich Smith Jamie C. Martin, Kimberley Griffiths Little, Carolee Dean, Lois Bradley, Marissa Burt, Terry Lynn Johnson, Bettina Restrepo, Kathryn Burak, Eve Marie Mont, J. Anderson Coats, Carole Estby Dagg, Jenny Ruden, Carrie Harris, and Natalie Bahm helped shape what this book has become.

My online critique partners, Valerie Geary and Kate Bassett, know this book almost as well as I do. The time and wisdom they have lavished on it—and me—are treasures indeed.

Vaunda Micheaux Nelson, Uma Krishnaswami, Stephanie Farrow, and Katherine B. Hauth have taught me about quality work, commitment to craft, and devotion to one another. Thank you for inviting this fledgling author into your well-established writing community.

My friends at High Desert Church offered tremendous support as this story unfolded, as did my running partner, Beth Benham, who kindly listened in on the process during our weekly runs.

I'd like to think I've shared the smallest taste of Alis's experience during my year as an exchange student in

Adelaide, South Australia. Much love to my sweet host family, the Mudges, who welcomed me as a daughter and sister.

I've thought often of Anna Ingwersen and Sergio Arias while writing about Kimi and Alis. These two filled my girlhood days with safe familiarity and endless creativity. Anna and Serg, thirty-plus years later, I'm proud to call you friends.

This book was a challenge on many levels, and I have drawn courage from my dear friend Jamie C. Martin, who reminded me that good work is often hard work. Thank you, Jamie, for everything.

My parents, Milt and Polly, and my sister, Chris, are pleased as punch to see me doing the very thing I set my heart on so many years ago. It's so good to have the three of you on my side.

Much love and gratitude goes to my husband, Dan, and our boys, Noah and Caleb, who make room for my head-in-the-clouds days, my fretting days, and those magical moments when everything comes together.

There are portions of history that are sad, inexplicable, even downright ugly. It was sometimes painful to study the events that happened at Roanoke so many years ago. Our world is a broken place, but I take great comfort in this promise: Someday God will redeem all things.